ROCKY THOMPSON

# Shadow of Helios

*Book 1 of the Solar Realms Saga*

OBSIDIAN
TOWER

First published by Obsidian Tower 2025

First edition

ISBN (paperback): 979-8-9999488-1-6
ISBN (hardcover): 979-8-9999488-2-3

This book was professionally typeset on Reedsy.
Find out more at reedsy.com

*To my wife and children, the dreamers who refuse to stay grounded. The rebels, outcasts, and driven minds who see the stars as possibilities to be reached.*

# Contents

# Acknowledgments

To my beta readers: you braved the labyrinth, survived the trials, and still came back with notes. Thank you for spotting the cracks, pushing me to dig deeper, and helping me carry this story across the finish line. If Kaelen had a soil pouch for each of you, it still wouldn't capture how much your feedback grounded this book.

# THE INVITATION

I t was on a Tuesday when the letter arrived.

Tucked inconspicuously in a bundle of his father's mundane diplomatic correspondence, comprising trade agreements, solar tariffs, and memos. All stamped with the increasingly irrelevant seal of the Earth Delegation. He would have missed it completely had it not been for the overly ornate gold leaves glinting along the edges of the envelope, a flourish too archaic for modern communication.

It was the only one addressed to Kaelen Voss.

The name looked foreign to him in that context, nestled among symbols of power. Not Aldren Voss, Envoy of Earth, but Kaelen. Just Kaelen. For a breath, the room seemed to narrow; the air gone still with anticipation he hadn't invited.

He was the quiet sort. Tall and slender, with a strength that came from long hours of study rather than sport. His gray eyes, often half-hidden beneath a loose fall of dark hair, carried a reflective weight uncommon for someone barely twenty. Nothing about him suggested a competitor.

Not yet.

The Voss estate, by design, was perched on the outskirts of New Alexandria's Diplomatic Quarter. A marvel of quiet opulence with its steel-veined marble, terraced gardens, and high-arched ceilings echoing with the soft hum of environmental regulators. The architecture

1

spoke of influence passed down in blood and favor.

Kaelen, as usual, sat hunched over a datapad in his father's study, the late afternoon sun filtering through reinforced glass and painting long shadows across the polished stone floor. His lean frame was folded into a chair too rigid for comfort, his brows furrowed as he studied the socio-economic impacts of hydroponic farming on Ganymede. Numbers made sense. They never asked for more than what he could give.

There was no warning. No premonition. Just an envelope and a seal.

Kaelen picked it up, his eyes lingering on the looping script beneath the crest of the Interplanetary Council. The wax shimmered faintly, highlighting the nine spheres locked in orbit around a golden flame. As he broke it, a sudden chill ran through his body, as though something within had cracked at the same time.

He read the contents once to himself. Then again, aloud. The words tasted foreign on his tongue.

"Kaelen Voss, by unanimous decision of the Council's Selection Committee, you are invited to present yourself as a candidate in the forthcoming selections to determine Earth's representative in the upcoming Interplanetary Ascendance..."

The letter dropped from his fingers, landing on the desk as if it had scorched him.

The ornate script spelled out more than an invitation... it was a summons. A demand. A trap dressed up as an honor.

The Interplanetary Ascendance: a pan-solar spectacle held once every ten years. The Games, as they were more commonly called, tested athletic prowess, strategic cunning, and technological innovation. A grand affair for the system's best and brightest.

The victor, the ultimate champion, would not only be showered with honors but awarded a seat on the Interplanetary Council, the very table that kept the fragile, century-old peace between the nine inhabited worlds of the Sol Realm barely intact.

He went pale, followed by an icy dread creeping into his usually placid demeanor. For a brief moment, Kaelyn did not recognize the room. It felt as if the walls of the study, once so familiar, so safe, were beginning to lean inward.

His father, Aldren Voss, a titan in Earth's diplomatic corps, would no doubt be thrilled. And that alone made Kaelen nauseous.

He had never expected to be chosen. He remembered the night he had submitted the application. Half-asleep, he hovered over the terminal while his father waited silently across the room. It had felt like signing a treaty with no clauses in his favor. Just a file uploaded into the void, a box ticked under the weight of expectation.

He was content with being the ambassador's son. He had no taste for glory. No hunger for power. He preferred the quiet hum of his datapads displaying the intricate patterns of agricultural optimization, the comfort of root systems and chlorophyll cycles, and the solitude of a world that didn't ask him to perform.

He was a scholar, content with being in the shadow of his own company.

He had always believed that true power was quiet. That the ones who sought the spotlight had already lost something essential. Maybe that was naïve. Maybe now he'd find out.

This wasn't a shadow. This was a stage with searing lights and relentless eyes. A maelstrom of political intrigue, weaponized media, and performance masquerading as diplomacy.

It was everything he had spent his life avoiding.

It's true: the years spent accompanying his father on diplomatic assignments had given him a passing fluency in politics. He could read a room, navigate layered courtesies, and even parry a veiled threat or two when necessary. But none of that had ever stirred ambition within him. Only awareness. Only caution.

His fingers drummed at a fast-paced cadence on the desk while his mind raced. He imagined the council chamber with its ring of planetary banners, each representative more calculating than the last. How many of them had reviewed his name? Had they seen potential? Promise?

Or had they simply seen his father?

Earth's seat on the Council had grown precarious over the past decade, more ceremonial than strategic. Too soft to intimidate, too proud to admit it. Maybe that's why they'd chosen him. A Voss. A legacy. Familiar. Harmless.

He stood at the window; the letter clutched in one hand, the sky outside dimming into hues of violet and ash. His reflection stared back at him in the glass. A boy too young. Too unsure.

Too visible.

Behind him, the slow, deliberate footsteps of Aldren Voss echoed through the hall, measured and unmistakable, like a verdict.

"You read it, then?" Aldren's voice was low but steady, carrying the authority of someone used to shaping the outcomes of planets.

Kaelen didn't turn around. "You already knew?"

"I was informed hours ago." A pause. "I wanted to wait until you found the letter."

Kaelen's jaw tightened. "Why? So you could watch me squirm?"

Aldren moved beside him, his sharp features softened by the fading light. "To see if you would run," he said, almost playfully.

Kaelen gave a humorless breath of laughter. "And what would you have done if I had?"

"I would have stopped you," Aldren said without hesitation.

The silence that followed was the kind only they knew. It was a dense, intimate and unresolved kind of silence. It had always lived between them, a thing they'd never dared to speak of. Kaelen couldn't help but remember the first time Aldren had left him behind on a diplomatic trip. There was no explanation, no goodbye. Just a schedule reshuffled and a door that never opened.

4

"I didn't expect to be chosen," Kaelen admitted. "I only applied because..."

"Because you thought it would earn my approval," Aldren finished. "I never asked for obedience, Kaelen. I wanted to see something true in you... something steady. The Council saw it. Even if you're not ready to."

Kaelen finally turned. "I don't want to be a symbol."

"No one ever wants to be," Aldren said quietly. "But sometimes the world decides for us, regardless of whether or not we're ready."

Kaelen didn't reply. The words were too close to being true.

Aldren left with a nod, and Kaelen lingered at the window, watching the light bleed out of the sky.

His bedroom felt colder than usual. The soft blue glow of his experimental fluorescent plants bathed the walls in muted light, but even they seemed dimmed somehow.

He lay awake for what felt like hours, eyes open to the dark. A part of him waited for the day to unravel, to reveal itself as a dream. But morning came anyway.

The days that followed passed like a slow unraveling.

The estate, once a constant murmur of meetings and diplomatic briefings, felt quieter than usual, as if the walls themselves were waiting for him to speak. Kaelen avoided the central halls where his father worked and spent most of his time wandering the terraced gardens and gravel paths that overlooked the cliffs beyond.

It was early autumn, and the wind carried with it the scent of distant fires and rain-washed stones.

He could breathe better outside, where no one was watching.

It was on the third day that his mother found him, seated beneath the old Varian tree near the southern courtyard. He didn't hear her approach. She had a way of moving quietly, like she didn't want to disturb the natural order of things.

5

"Your father said you accepted," she said, not accusing, not surprised. Simply stating it.

Kaelen nodded, still watching the wind ripple through the grass. "I didn't say no."

She sat beside him, folding her hands in her lap. Elara Voss had always been the gentler half of the diplomatic duo, quiet where Aldren was commanding, perceptive where he was forceful. There was steel in her, but it was buried beneath warm soil.

"He means well," she said after a moment. "But he doesn't always remember that being brave and being willing are not the same thing."

Kaelen looked at her, surprised.

"You've always been brave, Kael," she continued. "Even when you were small. But you were never one to look for the center of the room. That's not a weakness."

"Feels like one," he muttered. "Like I'm pretending to be someone I'm not just to keep up."

Elara smiled, bittersweet. "Pretending is what we do until we become. That's how most of us survive the beginning of anything important."

They sat in silence; the wind whispering through the tree's long branches. Somewhere in the distance, the sea broke against the cliffs.

"You don't have to win their games," she said softly. "But don't hide in them either."

Kaelen turned toward her. "And if I don't belong?"

"Then make a space where you do," she replied, her voice firm. "Not for them. For you."

That night, Kaelen stood in his room long after midnight, bathed in the soft pulse of the ambient wall lights.

The estate was silent.

His travel kit sat half-packed at the foot of his bed, its contents arrayed with clinical precision. A pair of utility boots. Modular garments. A biometric scanner. A sealed pouch of Earth soil his mother

6

had quietly placed beside the case earlier, her only explanation a small, knowing smile.

He picked it up, feeling its weight in his palm. Somehow, that handful of dirt felt heavier than the entire Council.

He folded each item deliberately, memorizing them as if anchoring himself to something real. A pair of old gloves. A pen from childhood. The data module sat untouched.

He sat on the edge of his bed and stared at his hands, calloused from his studies and the soil, not war, and whispered into the dark:

"Will I recognize myself when this is over?"

Outside, a sky ferry rumbled across the stars, trailing vapor like a scar across the night. His mind drifted, picturing them all; his future rivals. Martian tacticians raised on war simulators, Jovian survivalists shaped by pressure and stone, engineered prodigies and enhanced strategists from different corners of the universe. Titans, and weapons, and wonders.

And then there was him.

With soil under his fingernails and a head full of crop efficiency ratios.

The next morning, Kaelen rose before dawn.

The estate was already awake without him. His travel kit was complete, prepared by the attendants. He moved through the familiar halls in silence, brushing his fingers along the cold stone one last time.

In the foyer, Aldren waited.

"You'll be met by a representative from the Council's Orientation Division. They'll take you to the evaluation facility on Luna," Aldren said without preamble.

Kaelen nodded.

A moment passed. Then another.

Aldren stepped forward and placed a hand on his son's shoulder.

"Make them see you, Kaelen. Not me."

It was the closest thing to warmth he'd ever felt from his father. And for a fleeting second, the weight on his chest eased.

"I'll try," Kaelen said.

"No, son. Don't just try," Aldren said. "Be undeniable."

Kaelen stepped out into the shuttle bay, the rising sun catching the edges of the departing craft.

For the first time in his life, he wasn't leaving in his father's shadow. He was stepping into his own storm.

The doors to the transport hissed shut behind him, sealing Earth and everything familiar on the other side of the polished hull. Kaelen took a seat by the viewport, watching as the sky turned from amber to black, his reflection swallowed by stars. Whatever awaited him on Luna, it was already in motion. The life he'd known was receding with the gravity behind him.

The shuttle broke through the wispy upper atmosphere of Luna, Earth's gray, cratered satellite, and descended toward the sprawling compound nestled within the Mare Imbrium. From above, the facility looked almost like a scar carved into the surface; all sharp geometry and gleaming towers, its lines too precise to be anything but governmental.

Kaelen disembarked under the sterile wash of artificial lights, the dome shielding him from the desolate vacuum beyond. Everything here felt too quiet, too controlled, like a place built not just to host brilliance, but to contain it.

An attendant in Council-blue greeted him without a smile, issued his temporary access band, and led him to a private dormitory in the candidate housing wing. The quarters were modest, with one bed, one desk, and a sealed viewplate that simulated starlight. The walls were cold, but efficient.

Once alone, Kaelen dropped his bag by the bed and sat on the edge of the mattress. The silence pressed in like gravity. The datapad on the desk pulsed with unread messages: orientation schedules, evaluation protocols, psychological preparation materials. He ignored them for now.

Instead, he laid back and stared at the simulated sky, pondering his situation.

This was no longer hypothetical. No longer a paper application meant to satisfy his father. The path ahead had teeth now. He imagined his rivals once more. All sharpening themselves into weapons for the Council's approval.

And here he was. A scholar in a soldier's arena.

His fingers traced the edge of the access band at his wrist, a slender strip of metal and light that hummed faintly with encoded data.

He closed his eyes, but sleep did not come easily. The walls might have been soundproofed, but Kaelen could still hear the future breathing on the other side of them.

# SELECTIONS

T he process had been as unforgiving as it was public. A series of exhaustive psychological assessments and physical trials had narrowed thousands of hopeful candidates to a mere handful. Each test felt more like a performance than an evaluation; equal parts scrutiny and spectacle.

Kaelen found himself answering philosophical paradoxes while suspended in magnetic restraints and debating ethical dilemmas mid-combat simulation. At one point, he was asked whether loyalty or logic should guide leadership. He replied dryly that either could fail spectacularly if misapplied with confidence. The evaluators wrote something down. He suspected it wasn't admiration.

Each candidate's past was dissected. Their potential, as well as their every latent impulse, was sliced open beneath algorithmic scrutiny. Kaelen's lineage and his father's considerable influence had opened doors, but it had also placed a heavier burden on him. He wouldn't merely represent himself if chosen. He would stand as a living testament to Earth's diplomatic prestige, an avatar of soft power dressed in regulation armor.

So, he treated it all like he would an academic inconvenience: he would complete the coursework, submit the required answers, and hopefully return to obscurity. He hadn't given the trials the same painstaking focus he lavished on his research. To him, it was a public ritual, an exhausting formality to endure before resuming a quieter life.

The selection process was broadcast throughout the entire system. It was a grand spectacle meticulously orchestrated for maximum impact. Nine candidates, each of them a living embodiment of their planet's pride and aspirations, sat in solemn rows upon ornate thrones, arrayed before the full authority of the Interplanetary Council. Every breath seemed to echo within the vast banquet hall, the very air charged with centuries of rivalry, ambition, and the crushing gravity of history.

It was more than a ceremony; it was a declaration to all who watched that the fates of worlds might pivot on the chosen few.

One by one, each chosen competitor's name was called. Kaelen was only half paying attention when his name rang out, a stark, echoing announcement that shattered the fragile order of his world.

For an instant, he froze. He imagined headlines already being written, Aldren's unreadable face behind some conference table, his mother's quiet eyes watching the broadcast from their estate. He imagined tripping on his way to the podium and becoming a meme transmitted across nine worlds. His stomach tightened, breath shallow.

Hesitating at first, he rose slowly on unsteady legs, heart hammering against his ribs, as the towering holographic projections of the Council cast elongated shadows across his face. Billions of unseen eyes pressed down upon him, each moment of hesitation, each flicker of emotion laid bare beneath their silent judgment. Cameras locked onto him with merciless, unblinking precision, recording his every breath, every tremor in his hands.

When the adrenaline and shock of it all subsided, reality settled in its place like a slow, suffocating tide. Official notifications arrived in precise, impersonal streams: schedules, mandatory briefings, biometric calibrations, lists of expectations and obligations so extensive they felt almost punitive.

Kaelen moved through each appointment in a daze, haunted by the weight of what was to come. Nights offered no refuge; sleep fractured under the strain of racing thoughts and phantom voices whispering of futures he could neither predict nor control. By the time he surfaced from his stunned drift, the machinery of the Games had already claimed him.

What followed was a blur of rigorous training, politicized posturing, and a relentless cascade of media engagements that Kaelen classified as a new form of psychological warfare. He was swept into a rotating cycle of press conferences, panel interviews, and photo ops where he was expected to look both dignified and relatable... a nebulous requirement that clearly meant something to the public relations team but remained entirely alien to him.

On one occasion he was asked to pose in a hydroponics bay, cradling a tomato vine as though he'd nurtured it himself. Another time they made him stand beside a simulated mining rig in full gear, smiling as though labor hardship were a novelty. He held the shovel, he wore the expression, and all the while he wondered how long it would take for the "authentic Kaelen" to be replaced entirely by this storyboard version.

Each question lobbed his way felt less like an inquiry and more like a surgical strike engineered to expose his convictions, insecurities, or hidden ideologies. The goal, it would seem, was not to understand him, but to package him. Kaelen suspected that his "authentic self" was being work-shopped by committee.

He struggled with the growing realization that he was no longer simply Kaelen Voss, scholar, amateur agronomist, reluctant inheritor of a diplomatic legacy. He had become something else entirely: a walking symbol, a sanitized ideal projected across star systems, hair always slightly too styled, answers always slightly too rehearsed.

In private, he began referring to himself as Public Kaelen; a persona with a fixed jawline, a practiced smile, and an innate talent for saying precisely nothing in response to everything. The real Kaelen, the one who once spent nights charting crop yield algorithms for fun, now watched from behind the glass like a man peering at a creature that only vaguely resembled him.

His training regimen was brutal, a calculated assault on both body and mind that left Kaelen wondering if the Council's true goal was to crown a champion or simply see who survived long enough to regret applying. Endurance drills pushed him past nausea into what he privately dubbed "phase two" of physical despair, where his limbs trembled like overcooked noodles and his body gave out in artistic collapses onto alloy floors. The instructors called it conditioning. He called it a tragic misunderstanding of human limitations.

Combat training was worse. Merciless hand-to-hand sequences blurred together in a symphony of bruises, his ribs and arms rapidly becoming a gallery of failed counters. His opponents struck with precision and speed that left him in a constant debate over whether to block or just try not to scream creatively. Simulated battlefields offered no reprieve. Live-fire conditions triggered Kaelen's latent allergy to pain and poor odds. The acrid tang of ozone clung to his lungs like disappointment as holographic adversaries lunged with unrelenting menace.

Physically, he struggled. Raw strength and instinctive speed weren't exactly in his portfolio, unless one counted brisk walking and enthu-siastic sarcasm as athleticism. But where brute force failed, ingenuity quietly thrived. His analytical mind latched onto patterns like a predator onto prey, dissecting tactical puzzles with clinical precision. He mapped feints, shifts in weight, and behavioral tells as if solving an aggressive mathematical equation.

When opponents lunged with reckless power, he sidestepped with quiet calculation. He didn't win often, but when he did, it was with the satisfying grace of someone who'd memorized the entire game three moves ahead. In the cold geometry of combat, amid data overlays and probability matrices, Kaelen found the only comfort this ordeal offered: control, fleeting but earned.

Some nights he limped back to his quarters with bruises blossoming like dark constellations across his ribs. He refused medical intervention when he could hide it. The thought of his weakness being logged on some report made him grind his teeth harder than the pain itself.

Beyond the rigors of training, Kaelen began compiling quiet observations of his rivals; a mental dossier built not from reports or stats, but the charged subtleties of posture and silence.

Mars's representative walked like a warhead in human form, eyes sharp enough to cut steel, every breath measured and lethal. Neptune's moved with unsettling calm, a creature of chill calculations and half-finished smiles, like someone perpetually withholding a crucial variable. Saturn's candidate seemed to drift more than walk, vanishing between training rotations only to resurface with unnerving insights and an irritating habit of chewing data wafers mid-sentence.

The others offered only fragments: Jupiter's delegate exuded immovable confidence, like someone who hadn't considered failure a viable outcome, but their booming laughter after a rival botched a simulation suggested arrogance could be cracked.

Mercury's aura was quieter, coiled like a spring held under careful tension. Venus brought an elegant charisma that never quite hid the gleam of danger. Uranus remained unreadable, an enigma wrapped in perfect stillness. And Pluto... Pluto's delegate rarely spoke. But when they did, it was with the cold clarity of someone thinking five layers deeper than everyone else.

Kaelen noted them all without judgment, just a growing awareness that these weren't merely competitors. They were reflections of planetary will, akin to tools, weapons, and emissaries. Victory here wouldn't be decided by brute strength or charm alone. It would be decided in the moments no one saw coming.

Their early interactions were rehearsals in controlled ambiguity. Formal greetings were exchanged with military precision: tight nods, empty pleasantries, and handshakes so carefully measured they felt like choreographed sparring matches. Kaelen couldn't decide if he was attending a diplomatic summit or the prelude to a knife fight.

No one trusted anyone. That much was clear. Each competitor maneuvered as if they'd already seen the endgame and were now working backward from checkmate. Even their small talk had a disarming quality. The kind that left Kaelen wondering if he'd just been complimented or subtly threatened.

Kaelen kept to observation, his silence mistaken for aloofness by some and weakness by others. In truth, he was cataloging. Not just who these people were, but what they represented; the distilled essence of planetary identity and ambition. Strength came in many forms: some sharp-edged, others elegantly disguised.

And yet, amid the veiled threats and strategic silence, something unexpected stirred. It wasn't trust, not yet, but it felt like possibility. That perhaps even among rivals engineered for conflict, something more enduring might flicker into being. Not an alliance. Not friendship. But the faint beginnings of understanding. The only thing Kaelen thought might be worth more than victory.

The competitors moved in formation under escort, a slow procession through the vast expanse of the Lunar launch terminal, a monument to polished alloy and political theater. Reinforced glass arched overhead, revealing the stark black canvas of space punctuated by distant stars, while sleek banners of the Interplanetary Council hung motionless in the recycled air, each emblem a reminder of the power that watched them all.

Security personnel lined every walkway in a silent gauntlet of authority, visors opaque, expressions unreadable, hands resting near sidearms with practiced stillness. Their presence was not just protection; it was performance. A message. You are being watched, and none of you are in control.

Kaelen walked in silence among the other candidates, his footfalls echoing against the polished flooring like a ritual drumbeat. His throat felt tight, palms damp against the fabric of his uniform. He practiced neutrality with every step, the diplomatic mask drilled into him since boyhood, but inside his nerves thrummed like live wires.

Conversations were minimal, hushed, and clipped. A few murmured comments about the gravity dampeners or the eerie lack of music peppered in for substance. One delegate from Jupiter muttered, "They could at least pretend this wasn't a funeral march." Another replied dryly, "Depends whose funeral you expect it to be." A smirk passed between them like contraband.

Kaelen kept his expression neutral but clocked everything. Tones, glances, reactions. Years of navigating diplomatic receptions had taught him where the real tension lived: in what people didn't say.

When the sleek silhouette of their transport finally came into view, lit dramatically by docking floods, it felt less like an invitation and more like a challenge. The ship gleamed with unsettling precision. An elongated hull, seamless plating, the kind of design that whispered of wealth, power, and secrets too expensive for transparency. It hovered like a blade just before the plunge.

Boarding was conducted in silence, no pomp, no farewell speeches. Just retinal scans, identity confirmations, and the low hiss of sealed airlocks. Inside, the ship exuded sterile luxury: alloy panels, recessed ambient lighting, and hallways that curved like veins within a mechanical beast.

Kaelen couldn't help but feel that once the doors closed, they would no longer be competitors preparing for a contest. They would become cargo sealed inside a pressure vessel; highly volatile, tightly monitored, and just waiting for ignition.

# SOLARIS

The Solaris cut through the void with a silent grace; its silver plating adjusted to a smooth approximation of Earth standard. But there was nothing familiar about life aboard the vessel. It was not a home, not even a temporary one. It was a pressure chamber dressed in diplomatic polish. Every corridor, every lounge, and every meal felt like a stage for calculated maneuvering.

Even the air felt curated, scrubbed of personality and replaced with something sterile and faintly metallic. The hum of the drives reverberated just beneath perception, a constant pulse that Kaelen could feel through the soles of his boots, like a distant heartbeat belonging to something vast and mechanical.

As the transport drifted further from Earth's gravitational embrace, Kaelen found himself finally face to face with the diverse assembly of chosen champions without the buffer of protocol. And he would quickly learn that silence was not the same as peace.

The competitors moved through the ship like pieces on a chessboard, testing boundaries without ever saying them aloud. Seating choices in the common lounge became acts of silent declaration. The Martian delegate, Lyra Tal, always sat facing the entrance. Was it a soldier's instinct.... or perhaps a warning?

Neptune's delegates, with their crystalline implants glinting under the ambient lights, rarely spoke but always watched. The Venusian pair floated through social spaces like dancers through smoke, all charm and coiled grace, deflecting questions with poise and easing tension with a practiced touch that felt as strategic as any weapon.

Kaelen kept to the periphery, observing with care. He was no social tactician, but he understood dynamics. Years of shadowing his father through countless banquets, tense councils, and whispered backroom dealings had taught him exactly how these games were played.

He took notice of who deferred to whom in conversation, who changed the subject when Pluto's name came up, who laughed too easily and who never laughed at all. It was a kind of soft warfare, cloaked in pleasantries and exchanged beneath crystal carafes of carefully rationed wine. A language of controlled gestures and unspoken pacts; one he understood far better than he ever wished to.

There were briefings, of course. Monotone and coldly efficient, the orientation modules were broadcast through the ship's neural hubs. Filled with predictive modeling, past Games breakdowns, survival metrics, contingency scenarios. Each one served as a subtle warning: You are not prepared. You will be tested beyond imagination. And no one will save you but yourself.

Kaelen noticed the modules' emphasized being adaptive over skillful. How success wasn't measured in victories, but in endurance. The unspoken truth: the Games weren't designed to celebrate brilliance. They were designed to expose what broke first.

No one knew what the first trial would be, only that the Games rarely waited long. Suspicion, Kaelen realized, was a language all its own aboard the Solaris, and from what he could tell, everyone was fluent.

Adding to their discomfort, immediate whispers of conspiracy wound its way through the rank and file like dark currents in deep water, unseen but palpably felt. There were murmurs of sabotage cloaked as accidents, of clandestine pacts struck in shadowed corridors, of motives reaching far beyond individual glory. The seeds of future betrayal had already taken root, threading through the fragile alliances and setting each of them on edge.

The Solaris thrummed with a quiet, contained energy. Its polished chrome corridors mirrored the unease of its passengers, each delegation a living microcosm of its world. The observation deck had become a theater of silent posturing, each competitor embodying the pride and ambition of their home world.

Lyra of Mars stood near a towering viewport; her stance coiled with a predator's vigilance, as if waiting for the slightest provocation to strike. When she thought no one was watching, her fingers flexed restlessly. A tic, or perhaps a reminder that she still had control of her own body.

Theron of Neptune floated like a phantom between discussions; each faint nod a calculated maneuver, his cool detachment masking layers of quiet strategy. Kaelen noticed a flicker of emotion. An imperceptible tightening of his jaw when the conversation turned to planetary resource quotas. It was slight, so much so that anyone else might have missed it.

Jax of Saturn moved among technical crews and ship's personnel with quiet, unobtrusive ease, hands often folded behind his back or lightly brushing across data readouts. He rarely spoke, his silences carrying a subtle gravity that made even seasoned engineers glance up in wary respect. Yet his eyes missed nothing, cataloging every conduit and console with a sharp, assessing interest that suggested he was already re-configuring the ship in his mind.

There was no careless charm here, only a calm, penetrating watchfulness; the quiet certainty of someone whose understanding of systems ran so deep they no longer needed words to dominate a room.

Kaelen watched them all with measured care. The way one might study volatile elements poised on the brink of reaction. He'd seen diplomats feign politeness before, but never with such lethal undertones.

The Solaris dining hall was a muted space of neutral alloys and soft lighting, designed more for controlled civility than comfort. At the far end, an expansive viewport framed the stars in perfect stillness, unbothered by the shifting tensions gathering beneath them. Even the meals carried tension: quiet forks, strategic glances, nervous jokes that rarely landed. Every interaction was part reconnaissance, part performance.

Kaelen arrived late, tray in hand, scanning the quiet clusters of competitors seated at long metal tables. Most chose silence or kept to their own factions, but one table stood out as a rare convergence of planetary rivals. Lyra sat upright, shoulders squared as if she were still in armor. Jax flanked her left side, hunched over a deconstructed ration pack. He seemed more interested in re-purposing it than eating his food, soldering an interface chip into the utensil dispenser between bites. Across from them, Selene stirred a steaming drink with unhurried grace, while Mira leaned slightly back, her pale eyes flickering with detached curiosity.

Khel caught Kaelen's gaze and gave a slight nod; the closest thing to an invitation he was going to get. Taking a steadying breath, Kaelen joined them.

"Didn't think Earth would send a thinker. Figured they'd pick someone flashier."

Kaelen met his gaze evenly. "I suppose you'll have to adjust your expectations."

Khel chuckled. "Fair. But keep your wits about you, Voss. This ship's more dangerous than it looks."

Kaelen lifted his glass. "I noticed. Do you talk to everyone like that, or am I special?"

"Only the ones who might make it to the end."

The exchange ended with a nod, not of agreement, but of recognition. Not trust. Just... acknowledgment.

"You missed the fireworks," Mira said lightly, gesturing toward Lyra with her cup. "We were just debating the merits of militarism versus diplomacy."

"Debating?" Selene's voice was smooth as polished stone. "I'd call it strategic posturing."

Lyra didn't look up. "I don't posture. I prepare."

Kaelen set his tray down while trying to read the currents beneath the surface. "What's the context?"

"Helios," Mira replied. "And whether it's a proving ground or a pressure valve."

"Pressure valve?" Kaelen echoed.

"To release tension before it explodes... let them fight in an arena instead of in their home worlds. Keeps the Council clean."

Jax finally looked up. "That's a cynical interpretation."

Mira shrugged. "Not cynical. Practical."

Kaelen turned to Lyra. "And what do you think it is?"

"A test," she replied simply. "Of who's willing to do what the others won't."

"You mean survive," Kaelen said.

Lyra met his eyes for the first time. "No. I mean, win."

The table went silent for a moment.

Selene took a careful sip of her drink, her green eyes glinting. "And what defines winning, exactly? Endurance? Intelligence? Influence?"

"Control," Lyra said flatly.

"Control without sustainability breeds collapse," Selene countered. "I've seen it. Venus thrives because we understand when to yield and when to influence from beneath the surface."

"You call that thriving?" Lyra's smile was sharp. "I call it stagnation in silk."

Selene's gaze didn't flinch. "And I call your Mars a hammer with no sense of the material it strikes."

The air thickened. Kaelen's diplomatic instincts screamed to intervene before the tension could harden into something unfixable.

"So," he said evenly, "if this is more than spectacle, if it's meant to shape leadership qualities, what kind of leader is the system really looking for?"

"That depends," Mira murmured, brushing a silver strand behind her ear. "On whether the system wants to survive... or be replaced."

Jax gave Kaelen a brief, knowing look. "Now that's a more interesting question."

Kaelen nodded slowly, already sensing the fractures. This wasn't a team. It wasn't even a group. It was a gathering of weapons, each forged differently, each already testing the angles of the others' edges.

He could read rival ambitions and layered secrets in all of them, each faction carrying the weight of their world's expectations like invisible armor. They were more than competitors; they were living strategies, precisely engineered for advantage, and Kaelen found himself the sole observer mapping out the subtle architecture of their dangers.

Compared to the others, the Terran delegation felt like a quiet skiff drifting among warships. Diplomatic and composed, but painfully outmatched.

Kaelen's own unease deepened with every encounter, amplified by the intensity radiating from his fellow competitors.

He felt fragile in their presence, like a finely made porcelain doll set among weapons of war. His upbringing had prepared him for negotiation tables and ceremonial halls, not for this collision of raw strength, sharpened minds, and living machines. And for the first time, the rules he'd spent his life mastering felt... irrelevant.

Solaris's journey was less of a transit and more of a choreographed ballet of political posturing. Alliances flickered and fractured like unstable stars. Subtle insults were exchanged with polished smiles, and whispers coiled through the corridors like venomous smoke.

Kaelen took it all in, analyzing every interaction, every subtle shift in tone or expression, quietly adapting to the rules of a game no one had taught him to play. He listened to the hushed negotiations behind half-closed doors, parsed the careful language of declarations made in passing.

He read the unspoken grammar of power: the glances that lasted a second too long, the calculated silences, the shifts in seating arrangements that meant more than entire speeches. In the shadows of Solaris, Kaelen Voss was putting together the pieces and beginning to understand the true nature of these so-called Games.

Aris of Mercury moved through Solaris like a whisper of heat before the flame. Quick, lean, and impossible to ignore once noticed. Kaelen caught sight of her slipping from one corridor to the next, always on the move, always alone. Her frame was wiry, built for speed and survival, and her deep-umber skin shimmered faintly under the ship's lighting like sun-baked copper. She rarely spoke, but when she did, her words came sharp and economical, carved from the same heat-forged logic that governed life on her volatile world.

He once overheard her in a strategy forum dismantling a delegate's proposal with clinical efficiency. No flourish. No ego. Just facts, laid bare like nerves.

"She doesn't posture," someone had whispered behind him. "She calculates the angles and decides if you're worth the breath."

And Kaelen, watching her expressionless profile fade into the crowd, believed it.

As the Solaris coasted toward Helios, its engines whispering like restrained thunder, Kaelen felt the first flicker of a new understanding settle deep in his chest. The Games hadn't yet begun... at least, not officially. But the competition had already started, and it wasn't just survival that was on the line.

It was the right to be seen as real in a world where everyone had already chosen which version of themselves to weaponize.

# JOURNEY TO HELIOS

O ver time, the very corridors that once buzzed with calculated exchanges and veiled alliances emptied. Exhaustion set in, wearing down even the most steadfast delegates until hushed councils dwindled and rival factions retreated to their private quarters to plot in guarded seclusion.

The observation deck, once a theater of poised diplomacy and barely restrained ambition, grew quiet. Conversations became murmurs lost to the ship's ambient hum, footsteps fewer, suspicious eyes less openly watchful. It was as if Solaris itself exhaled, drawing the players inward, leaving vast spaces for Kaelen to wander through alone.

In the long silences, the ship seemed to shift. The sterile lighting dimmed to cooler hues, casting ghostly shadows that stretched along the walls like fading echoes of previous days. The hum of the engines wavered now and then, taking on an irregular cadence. Something like a heartbeat out of rhythm, or whispering of faults that weren't truly there. Kaelen sometimes caught the faint vibration beneath his palms as if the ship were murmuring in its sleep.

He often found himself alone on the observation deck, surrounded by the cold sprawl of distant stars. He sought no strategy there, no careful reflection, only a rare stillness untainted by rivalry or expectation. Kaelen was a scholar; a diplomat's son shaped by measured words and quiet study. Yet in that vast, indifferent darkness, he wondered what kind of man he would need to become to endure the trials ahead, and whether he would recognize himself when it was over.

In the deepest hours of the shipboard stillness, Kaelen encountered Nox standing alone at the forward viewport. Draped in layered, iridescent fabric that shimmered faintly in the starlight, the representative from Uranus was a spectral figure. He was tall and spare, his lavender skin seeming almost translucent beneath the soft blue glow.

"You're searching for clarity," Nox said without turning. His voice was low, almost melodic, as though speaking to the stars themselves.

Kaelen hesitated slightly, then stepped closer. "And you aren't?"

Nox's geometric facial markings pulsed faintly with internal bio-light as he turned his head. "I look for patterns," he said. "Not answers. Answers are fragile things... Patterns endure."

There was no arrogance in his tone, only quiet observation. He had a presence one would think was shaped by conflict, not isolation. It was the kind that bred insight at the cost of warmth.

Kaelen frowned slightly. "And what pattern do you see now?"

Nox studied him for a long moment, eyes reflecting the distant stars. "A fracture line," he murmured. "Running straight through you. You are already breaking toward what you fear most."

Kaelen felt the words settle like cold water through his chest. "You speak as if you've seen this before."

Nox's expression was unreadable. "On Uranus, we learn to listen to things that break slowly."

The silence hung stretched in the air, neither uncomfortable nor kind. Kaelen sensed something vast and ancient behind that stillness; a wisdom too distant to weaponize. It left him unsettled... and slightly humbled.

The air aboard Solaris crackled with unspoken tension as Kaelen began encountering his rivals beyond the sterile briefings, orientations, and meals. Despite the ship's vast corridors, it felt oppressively close, a floating crucible where every glance and every word was weighed down with silent stakes.

While wandering the lower decks, Kaelen found Lyra alone in a secluded training bay, mid-motion, her body flowing through combat forms with lethal economy. Each strike and pivot was stripped of flourish; every breath measured for efficiency. The crimson of her uniform burned against the sterile white walls, the only sound the steady thud of her boots striking the deck in a mechanical cadence.

She didn't acknowledge him at first. But when her gaze finally slid to meet his own, it pinned him where he stood.

"Are you just going to watch?" She said, her tone clipped, "Or do you actually intend to learn something?"

Kaelen straightened. "Observation tends to precede strategy."

Lyra pivoted, driving her elbow into the air as if striking an invisible foe. "Strategy's worthless if you hesitate. Out there, hesitation gets you killed."

"So does charging forward without understanding your opponent."

She stopped, breathed in steadily, and stepped closer. "You'll either adapt or be a footnote. Don't expect warnings next time."

Her eyes held no overt hostility, only a cool, assessing curiosity. She was like a predator determining whether the movement before her was worth the chase. Kaelen suddenly felt small, like an insect under a magnifying glass. Beneath her precision, he saw the faintest flicker; a tremor in her gloved hand that might have been exhaustion... or fear. It vanished almost immediately. She'd learned early in her life to erase weakness... even from herself.

At that precise moment, Kaelen understood something about her: Lyra was not merely strong. She was ruthless, and she would shatter anything, or anyone, that stood in her way.

In the hours that followed, Kaelen found Theron in the ship's library, silhouetted by a silent cathedral of flickering data screens and filtered starlight. The Neydrin strategist sat alone, his long fingers moving with surgical precision across a scattered constellation of datapads, blue light painting his angular features in ghostly relief.

Theron didn't look up as Kaelen approached but spoke as though he were expecting him. "Probability matrices don't lie," he said, eyes fixed on a glowing schematic. "Mars and Saturn will over commit. Neptune waits. Venus divides."

Kaelen remained silent, studying the data swirling in Theron's halo of light. "And Earth?" he finally asked.

Theron's fingers stilled. He turned his gaze, glacial and unreadable. "Earth plays diplomacy. But in the end, every piece on the board gets used."

Kaelen exhaled slowly. "You speak as if the outcome has already been decided."

"It has," Theron replied, returning to his work. "You just haven't seen the board clearly yet."

Kaelen offered no retort, not for a lack of understanding but because there was no space to contradict. This wasn't a discussion; it was instruction. A glimpse into a mind that treated the Games as a vast, multi-layered chessboard where alliances dissolved at convenience and pawns existed to be sacrificed.

And yet, just before Kaelen left, Theron said quietly, without looking up, "When the first trial begins, trust your instincts, not the training. The Council loves the illusion of fairness."

Kaelen paused before stepping into the corridor's sterile silence, but Theron had already turned away, his focus consumed again by the luminous maze of probability. The advice lingered in Kaelen's mind like a code he wasn't yet ready to decrypt. It was as if Theron had already mapped his position, weighed his value, and consigned him to an outcome only he could see.

The hum of the ship pressed close, rhythmic and low, as though echoing the strategist's words: the illusion of fairness. He made his way back to his quarters through the dim, flickering light. The corridors felt narrower than before, every reflection of his face stretched thin in the polished alloy walls.

Inside, the room was silent except for the soft thrum of the life-support vents. Kaelen sat at the edge of his bunk, replaying the conversation in his mind. Theron's analysis had been cold, but beneath the logic was something more unnerving, a certainty that bordered on prophecy.

He wondered what kind of game board he'd been placed on. What piece was he meant to play?

Sleep came reluctantly, fractured by dreams of moving shapes and shifting lights, the sound of footsteps echoing in hallways that had no end. When he awoke, the lighting in his quarters had dimmed to the ship's false dawn, a pale blue glow seeping from the walls. His body felt heavy, his mind still caught between memory and motion.

He needed noise, something tangible, mechanical, something to drown out the calculations still whispering in his head.

Jax, the Satori engineer, was a study in understated brilliance, a stark foil to Lyra's coiled violence and Theron's cold precision. Kaelen stumbled upon him in the ship's engineering bay, surrounded by a chaotic sprawl of tools, half-rendered schematics, and softly glowing devices in various states of resurrection.

Jax barely acknowledged Kaelen's arrival, fingers working deftly on a dismantled conduit. Sparks flickered like fireflies around his hands. "That relay's misaligned," he muttered, not looking up. "Would've fried half the nav system mid-jump."

Kaelen raised a brow. "And you just fixed it with a pocket tool?"

"Tools don't matter," Jax said simply. "Only understanding the pattern."

Kaelen stepped closer, watching the rhythm of his movements. They

28

were methodical, unhurried, almost meditative. "You make it sound like the universe is mechanical."

"It is," Jax said. "The trick is to realize you're a part of the mechanism."

For a fleeting moment, Kaelen saw not detachment but faith, the quiet conviction of someone who found comfort in complexity. Jax didn't control systems. He belonged to them.

Jax finally looked up, his gaze flicking briefly toward Kaelen before returning to the conduit. "You think diplomacy will help you down there?"

Kaelen hesitated. "It's helped humanity survive this long."

A faint smirk ghosted across Jax's lips. "Surviving isn't the same as understanding."

He powered down his tools, the hum of the bay softening to silence. "You'll learn," he said, almost absently. "Everyone does eventually. Usually the hard way."

Kaelen watched him for a moment longer, unsure if the words were meant to be cynicism or encouragement. Jax had already turned back to his work, the reflection of his hands fractured across a dozen metallic surfaces, moving in perfect synchronization with the ship's pulse.

As Kaelen stepped out of the engineering bay, he realized he could still hear that rhythm echoing faintly behind him; steady, precise, indifferent.

Kaelen made his way to the mess hall, where he found Khel. He expected brute strength and got a miner-philosopher forged by pressure and patience. They shared a meal in silence at first. But after a while, Khel started opening up to him a bit and talked of his home, of storms that howled for weeks and the people who endured without complaint.

"Storms change you," Khel said, eyes distant. "But they also teach you when to hold your ground."

Kaelen nodded in agreement. "And when to move?"

Khel smiled faintly. "Aye. Even stone shifts if the pressure's right."

There was no grand philosophy, no threat, just the simple wisdom of a man who had weathered too much and survived. It humbled Kaelen more than all of Lyra's warnings and Theron's analyses combined.

Moments like that, the quiet ones, unraveled him more than threats ever could. He caught himself holding his breath, afraid that if he spoke, the moment's fragile humanity might vanish.

The ship's corridors grew quieter still. Where once there had been strategy whispered in corners and alliances inked in glances, now there was stillness. Everyone was waiting.

Kaelen wandered the halls of Solaris, absorbing the silence, feeling the weight of it. He often returned to the observation deck, no longer watching others but searching within. He wasn't sure yet who he'd become, only that survival alone wouldn't be enough.

Yet even amid those rare moments of connection, tension simmered beneath the calm. Every word carried weight; every gesture was calculated; suspicion coiled just beneath polished courtesies. Trust was a luxury no one could afford. Alliances flared and faded like unstable stars; fragile, fleeting constructs born of necessity, never conviction.

They were rivals, each bearing a distinct physical, intellectual, or political strength that made them potential allies or looming threats. Kaelen saw it now with a growing, clinical clarity: the real battle thrived in whispered bargains along dim corridors, in glances traded over shared meals, and in every carefully veiled threat and promise. It was a war—quiet, but relentless all the same.

In the quieter corners of Solaris, Kaelen began piecing together tentative understandings from fleeting exchanges and half-formed gestures. Khel's raw strength is tempered by honesty. Jax's precision mirrored his own diplomacy. These fragments hinted at fragile alliances and patterns forming beneath the noise.

His father's voice surfaced unbidden: People are puzzles, Kael. Solve them before they solve you.

Suspicion still clung to them all; it always would. Along with it, something else had taken root: an awareness of shared circumstance.

Once, in a dim maintenance corridor, Jax approached him without ceremony, slipping a small device into his hand. "Just in case you find yourself cornered," he murmured. His voice was flat, eyes already shifting away. It was offered not with warmth, but with the cool logic of a man who understood that leverage might one day flow both ways. Kaelen accepted it with a silent nod, uncertain whether this was the seed of mutual trust or merely an extension of Jax's quiet, inscrutable calculus.

The battlefield loomed ahead, and none of them would face it entirely alone. Lyra and Theron remained elusive, each cloaked in precision that betrayed nothing of deeper loyalties, their intentions as fluid as the quiet pacts being woven across mess halls and training bays. Victory, Kaelen realized, would demand far more than brute strength. It would hinge on navigating a labyrinth of ambition and deception that stretched well beyond the confines of any arena.

That night, as Solaris glided through the silent darkness, Kaelen felt the faint tremor of deceleration beneath his feet. A soft chime rippled through the decks. It was barely audible, yet heavy with implication.

The ship was slowing down.

Somewhere ahead, invisible beyond the viewport's veil of stars, the Helios station was awakening.

And the Games... were about to begin.

# THRESHOLD

The approach to Helios was nothing short of breathtaking. Hanging in the void like a second sun, the colossal structure of shimmering alloys and curved glass dominated the horizon, its surface ablaze with reflected solar light that dazzled and blinded by turns. A masterpiece of collaborative engineering, Helios stood as a testament to the Realm's ambition. It stood as a fragile symbol of hope, suspended between worlds, born of countless hands across contrasting planets.

As Solaris executed its final docking maneuvers, Kaelen felt both excitement and apprehension churn in equal measure. The Games were no longer an abstract specter; they loomed before him in hard metal and searing brilliance. Inside awaited an ever-shifting arena, a technological marvel capable of conjuring environments from every corner of the system. Each trial meticulously designed to strip away pretense, to test not only the body's endurance but also the mind's resilience, until all that remained was something raw and undeniably true.

The docking clamp engaged with a low, seismic thunk. As the airlocks cycled, Kaelen stared at his reflection in the polished viewport. He squared his shoulders and held a neutral expression, but he couldn't hide what was in his eyes, a shimmer that betrayed the tension thrumming beneath his calm. He wasn't afraid. Not yet. But the space between fear and awe was narrowing.

When he stepped across the threshold, the air aboard Helios struck him as different. It was cleaner, drier, and subtly pressurized. Gravity here pulled just a fraction heavier than Earth standard, as if to remind every arrival that Helios bowed to no single world's comfort. The hum of the station resonated deeper too, a bass undertone that vibrated in the bones more than ears. Every step felt weighted and deliberate.

The terminal linking Solaris to Helios buzzed with orchestrated chaos. There was a mesh of Council staff, security escorts, and planetary liaisons moving in precise synchrony.

For a moment, Kaelen's attention was pulled to a figure slightly out of formation, a nimble silhouette clad in the muted monochrome of a Plutonian operative. Nox.

He moved like a shadow that hadn't yet decided whether to cling to the floor or vanish entirely. His gaze, amber and flat, swept over the security checkpoint. Not with suspicion but with idle assessment, as though mapping weaknesses on instinct. Where others walked with purpose, Nox drifted, one hand brushing lightly along a wall panel as if feeling for something unseen. There was no defiance in it, no bravado, just the uncanny fluidity of someone who had spent too much time slipping between boundaries others didn't even see. Kaelen felt a prickle of wariness. Nox didn't observe people. He dissected them.

The first days aboard Helios passed in a blur of orchestrated chaos. Orientation briefings dissolved into labyrinths of logistics and a relentless parade of media scrutiny. Each competitor was ushered through interviews, press conferences, and meticulously staged photo opportunities. Spectacles crafted to spark fervor across the system.

His father's diplomatic shadow loomed large, lending him both unassailable legitimacy and a burden of expectation he could almost feel pressing into his spine. Despite his own quiet misgivings, Kaelen found himself swiftly crowned a media darling.

Between obligations, he found fleeting moments of solitude in the atrium overlooking the station's artificial day-night cycle. He watched the false sunlight arc across simulated skies, an illusion so perfect it almost hurt. These engineered rhythms were meant to comfort, but they only reminded Kaelen how far from Earth he truly was.

The air smelled faintly of ozone and sterilized metal, a manufactured perfection that felt like a lie. Beneath it all, he could sense the pulse of the station, steady and vast, as though the structure itself were alive and watching.

It wasn't long before he mastered the subtle architecture of public perception: the strategic pause that transformed silence into authority, a deft anecdote to steer away from probing questions, statements honed with just enough ambiguity to satisfy curiosity without ever truly revealing himself.

Each appearance left him empty. Every headline built a version of him that was clean, composed, impossible. Public Kaelen had followed him to Helios.

The orientation concluded in a sterile chamber of white light and polished steel. Holographic projectors displayed the names, roles, and planetary affiliations of each competitor. Kaelen's Terran insignia drew murmured attention, but it was the diplomatic tone of the Council representative—"Earth's legacy envoy"—that framed him differently than the rest.

As the groups dispersed, Kaelen drifted to the edge of the chamber, already feeling the burn of scrutiny trailing behind him. That's when he noticed a faint commotion near one of the exits. A heated exchange clipped short by a single, surgical phrase.

"No, I don't need clearance. I've already rerouted through the inner channel. Your approval is irrelevant."

Aris, clad in sleek military black, stood between two Martian delegates. Her expression was unreadable, but her posture was unyielding.

Her voice was dry and deliberate, with each word carrying the sharp precision of someone used to commanding order in the middle of chaos.

The Martians withdrew, irritated but outmatched, and Aris stepped forward into the corridor's light. Kaelen didn't miss the faint smirk tugging at the edge of her mouth as she passed him; a quiet storm barely restrained. She radiated presence not through bravado, but through sheer refusal to yield an inch of space to anyone.

He studied her briefly, committing the moment to memory. Aris wasn't just prepared for conflict; she expected it.

Shortly after, Selene intercepted him near the corridor's archway, her silhouette framed by Helios's rising synthetic light.

"You're adjusting quickly," she said, arms folded. "It's rare for someone with no military or technical distinction to dominate headlines."

Kaelen offered a diplomatic half-smile. "I wouldn't call it domination. Just visibility."

Selene stepped closer, her voice cool but edged. "Visibility is currency here. And some of us must bleed for every ounce."

He studied her for a moment, then nodded. "And others must balance between being admired and being feared. I imagine Venus taught you both."

Her eyes narrowed. "Don't patronize me, Terran. You're playing a game others have lived their entire lives preparing for."

"I'm not underestimating anyone," Kaelen said softly. "But I won't apologize for people noticing. Maybe it's not about proving who deserves attention; maybe it's about proving what you do once you have it."

Selene tilted her head slightly, reassessing. "We'll see if that philosophy holds when the Games begin. Attention fades. Power doesn't."

Then she turned and walked away, her stride unshaken. But her words lingered like static, resonating in the charged silence she left behind.

Kaelen remained standing there for a moment longer, the echo of her voice louder than the orientation briefing had been. He had expected strategy and strength. What he hadn't expected was how much the politics of performance would weigh on everyone, especially those like Selene, who bore the burden of both planetary expectation and personal scrutiny.

He realized then that fame made him visible but not known. It was a kind of isolation that mirrored the vacuum outside Helios; bright, infinite, and utterly silent.

The arena itself was a staggering feat of engineering ambition, vast enough to cradle entire ecosystems within its shifting walls. It could summon Martian canyons, sculpt ice plains to rival Neptune's bleak expanses, mimic the roiling tempests of Jupiter, or cast rings of fractured stone reminiscent of Saturn's haunting halos.

Every inch was a calculated ordeal, crafted to challenge not just the body's endurance, but the mind's capacity for adaptation and cunning. Kaelen stood beneath its soaring vaults, rendered silent by something deeper than fear; a profound reverence for what different cultures could achieve when united by a shared purpose, however tenuous.

The opening ceremony unfurled with dazzling precision: torrents of light and cascading sound, each planetary delegation arrayed in its finest, a living mosaic of pride and fragile alliances.

As Kaelen marched with the Terran contingent, the roar of unseen crowds surged over him like an ocean. The weight of expectation settled across his shoulders, heavy as a mantle woven from every hope and hushed desperation Earth still dared to hold.

He caught sight of his competitors in scattered glimpses, the cold determination of Lyra flanked by her Saturnian cohort, the graceful stillness of Mira radiating calm beside Neptune's delegation, the unwavering poise of Khel at Jupiter's side, his eyes already scanning the arena like a battlefield yet to be claimed. They were symbols and strategies, threats and promises, walking testaments to their worlds.

The ceremony's grandeur was overwhelming, but beneath the thunder of applause Kaelen could hear the quieter pulse of the station itself, the measured rhythm of the life systems, the faint hiss of reconfiguration panels behind the walls. It was as if Helios itself was alive, studying them, preparing itself for the battles ahead.

Around him, celebration and competition blurred into a single, dazzling spectacle. Yet the underlying expectations had never been starker. The Ascendance was far more than a gauntlet of manufactured hazards; it was a stage for declaring legacy, for testing diplomatic nerve, and for proving which worlds harbored the uncompromising will to survive.

Survival unfolded not only within the arena's shifting trials but in the careful maneuvering of ambitions, in the fragile calibration of alliances with every measured glance and quiet concession.

As Kaelen studied the arena's vast waiting heart, a quiet certainty settled over him: the true Games had yet to begin, and they would be played on far more fronts than mere terrain.

Beneath the thunderous applause, Kaelen's heartbeat matched the rhythm of the drums. For the first time, fear and purpose moved in tandem.

The weight of Earth, perhaps even greater now, rested squarely on his shoulders. He would have to learn quickly: when to trust, when to strike, and most critically, how to endure.

The days leading up to the official start blurred into a relentless rhythm of training, strategy sessions, and razor-edged observation. He scrutinized his competitors, cataloging not just their physical prowess but the nuances of their personalities, the subtle tells that betrayed calculation or concealed fear, the silent undercurrents that drove their choices.

Kaelen watched Lyra closely during combat drills; her strikes were delivered with merciless precision, eyes locked forward, a creature to whom hesitation or compassion simply did not exist. He listened to Theron's pronouncements, parsing the hidden architecture of each carefully placed word, feeling the manipulations ripple beneath that glacial calm. He examined Jax's prototypes with a mix of awe and apprehension, marveling at devices whose elegant design masked a chilling capacity to shift the tides of conflict without ever drawing blood.

Even in brief exchanges, Kaelen sensed how easily trust could be broken here, and how few truths would ever be spoken aloud.

In the end, he understood the Games would never be about glory alone. They were about endurance. About adaptation. About safeguarding the fragile hopes of an entire world that had dared to pin its future on him.

And that burden... He could feel it now, pressed into his spine with a weight that mimicked gravity itself, anchoring him to a destiny he still hadn't grasped....

# THE GAUNTLET

The weight of responsibility still coiled through Kaelen's chest as they were ushered forward. Before them, the Gauntlet loomed, a towering edifice of shimmering obsidian, pulsing faintly with latent energy. It wasn't merely a structure; it was a monument to both galactic ingenuity and sanctioned cruelty, a grim testament to the lengths the Ascendance Selection Committee would go to purge the unworthy.

The first trial, as they had been led to believe, would not only test their strength, but the synergy of their body and mind, a trial engineered to expose every weakness. Kaelen, despite his diplomatic heritage and strategic intellect, felt unprepared. Nothing could have readied him for the raw, unforgiving brutality of what lay ahead.

Kaelen's initial scan of the Gauntlet revealed a brutal sequence of interconnected challenges, each more punishing than the last. Tests of strength, endurance, agility, and intellect were woven together into a single, unrelenting onslaught of attrition. He turned his gaze to the others, noting how each prepared in their own telling way.

Lyra, the Redborn, honed her blades with ritualistic precision, every movement a study in lethal economy. Theron, ever composed, sat cross-legged before a drifting holo-schematic, lips moving in an inaudible murmur as he mapped probabilities and spun intricate webs of calculation.

Jax sat hunched over an array of crooning devices, his hands a blur as he fine-tuned tools that might twist chaos to his advantage. And Khel, towering and silent, radiated a humbling, immovable strength. He offered no visible preparation at all, only the calm assurance of a man who had weathered worse and simply endured.

The air in the transport bay vibrated with restrained energy. Kaelen could almost taste the ozone tang of charged systems, the way it mixed with the quiet, human scent of fear that no one dared to speak of. Someone to his left murmured a brief prayer. A simple and desperate tome from a forgotten time. The sound of it seemed to die too quickly in the sterile air.

Kaelen's lack of lifelong combat training was impossible to ignore. He didn't possess Lyra's raw, unflinching aggression or Khel's elemental strength, nor did he command Theron's glacial cunning. What he did have, what he had always relied on, was adaptability. Intellect. The ability to read patterns, anticipate subtle shifts, and improvise under pressure.

He heard his father's voice again, calm but unyielding on the night before his departure: "You won't win by force, Kaelen. That's not your strength. You win by knowing people. By thinking faster than they do. Let them play their games, just make sure you can still see the board."

Once dismissed as polished diplomatic platitudes, those words now settled around him like armor. He would not enter the Gauntlet as a warrior. He would face it as a strategist, determined not to overpower the trials, but to outmaneuver them.

The transport bay was silent, save for the low hum of magnetic rails guiding the chamber deeper into the heart of the Gauntlet. Kaelen stood with the others inside the reinforced observation capsule, its glass walls revealing shifting glimpses of obsidian corridors and flickering energy grids.

His fingers brushed a small pouch tied to his side, the one filled with soil his mother had given him. In its familiar weight, he found a steady rhythm. A reason to push forward. For a fleeting second, he let his eyes close. He pictured New Alexandria's terrace gardens, the way the wind moved through the leaves and the sunlight fractured through glass. The memory steadied him like gravity returning to a drifting body.

The mechanical tendrils of the arena stirred to life around them. At the capsule's center, a hologram flared to life, an elegantly robed figure, face obscured by a smooth, featureless mask, voice modulated to a calm, unnervingly pleasant register.

"Welcome, contenders," the Host intoned, each word measured and smooth as if rehearsed countless times. "In moments, you will be deployed into the Gauntlet's first environment. This phase will test your adaptability, your willingness to cooperate, or to outmaneuver. Terrain and objectives are randomized. Failure to complete the challenge will result in immediate elimination from the competition."

The Host inclined its masked head slightly. "Form alliances if you wish. Act alone if you dare. You will not be given second chances."

For an instant, the holographic figure seemed to linger, as if savoring some private amusement behind that smooth, unreadable mask. Then, just as abruptly, it vanished, leaving only a fading shimmer of light in the air. The capsule gave a slight jolt as it locked into an airlock chamber, magnetic seals hissing into place, the machinery oblivious to the uneasy silence that followed.

Across from Kaelen, Lyra rolled her shoulders and flexed her grip around the hilt of her blade, muscles coiling like a spring. Beside her, Theron didn't so much as blink, eyes already locked on the shifting data streams behind where the Host's hologram had hovered, as if trying to outguess the system itself. Jax quietly slipped a slim tool into his sleeve, movements economically precise. Khel cracked his knuckles without a word, jaw set, every line of his massive frame radiating silent focus.

Kaelen's heart thundered in his chest, but he held his ground. This wasn't panic. It was clarity, a sharpness honed by the quiet echo of his father's counsel: You don't need to be the strongest. You just need to be the last one still thinking.

A hiss of steam. The chamber lurched and began its slow descent. The Games had begun.

The chamber doors hissed open, releasing the contestants into the first trial: an immense cavern hollowed from the Gauntlet's inner walls. The environment was artificial but felt terrifyingly real. Jagged cliffs of black stone jutted outward, shot through with veins of glowing circuitry that crawled like molten arteries across the rock.

Narrow platforms stretched above a yawning chasm that pulsed with shifting light far below, each flicker hinting at unseen machinery—or worse. The air was thin and bitingly cold, every breath a raw reminder of the hostility engineered into this place. Every surface radiated the promise of sudden violence.

For a moment, Kaelen felt utterly insignificant. Like one small life staring into the immense, indifferent machinery of something designed to test the limits of sentience itself.

The first challenge was a trial of pure endurance, forcing them along a winding, treacherous path riddled with escalating physical obstacles. Towering climbing walls loomed ahead, their facades studded with jagged holds that threatened to shear skin from the bone. Rope bridges swung violently over yawning voids, each gust of chilled air turning them into pendulums of potential disaster.

Razor-thin ledges forced contestants to inch sideways, bodies flattened against sheer drops that plunged out of sight into shifting luminescence. The air hummed with raw exertion, filled with grunts, gasps, and the occasional scream ricocheting off steel-laced rock.

Kaelen moved with breath tight but controlled, advancing through caution rather than brute force. Where others relied on reckless leaps or sheer muscle, he paused at each junction, meticulously plotting routes that offered the best balance of stability and speed. He ducked beneath a platform just as it splintered behind him, shards clattering into the void, skipped an entire run of rungs that wobbled under the slightest weight, and avoided a rope bridge that groaned dangerously under Khel's massive frame. What Kaelen lacked in raw power, he made up for in precision. And in that deliberate calculation lay his unassuming edge.

As he climbed, he caught flashes of the others. Lyra's breath rasped like machinery as she scaled a vertical ridge; Theron moved with sharp, analytical efficiency until a misjudged leap cost him precious ground. The safety fields shimmered faintly at the periphery, more symbolic than protective, and somewhere above them a scream broke through the din, cut short too abruptly to be anything but final. A name flared red across a hovering holo-feed. One down.

Lyra, for all her formidable strength, faltered on a narrow ascent, momentum stalling at a deceptively shallow handhold that drained her leverage and left her clawing against the stone. Theron, calculating but overconfident, attempted a shortcut that demanded more brute force than he possessed; Kaelen caught it in his eyes just before the slip, the instant where intellect collided with the hard limits of flesh. This trial was no stage for domination. It was a crucible for survival. And Kaelen was surviving.

At last, the final ledge yielded to solid ground. Kaelen pulled himself over the rim, lungs searing, muscles trembling with spent effort. Around him, the others stumbled forward one by one, each bearing the raw stamp of exhaustion and the brittle relief of a narrow escape. There were no cheers, no triumph, only the quiet, shared knowledge that this was merely the first of many ordeals.

They regrouped in a dimly lit antechamber, breathless and bruised, bodies streaked with fresh scrapes and grime from the climb. No one met another's eyes for long; each was locked in private calculation, cataloging who faltered, who endured, and what it might mean for the trials ahead. Kaelen felt the ache burrow deep into his shoulders, a sharp reminder that endurance was as much about surviving the spaces between challenges as the tests themselves.

Nearby, Lyra flexed her hands with quiet frustration. Theron stood rigid, hiding the sting of his misstep behind a mask of icy disdain, and somewhere farther off, the indistinct murmur of distant machinery whispered that the Gauntlet was far from done with them.

The second phase shifted abruptly from punishing physical strain to cerebral warfare. The competitors stepped into a chamber awash in pale blue light, its walls alive with holographic interfaces and drifting glyphs that morphed and rearranged with each passing heartbeat. Here, brute strength was meaningless.

This was a trial of intellect, testing pattern recognition, memory, political nuance, and raw problem-solving ability. Kaelen's pulse steadied. This was his element.

Complex riddles blinked into existence, multi-layered logic puzzles demanding spatial reasoning, diplomatic insight, and the adaptability of someone accustomed to reading beneath layers of implication. Years spent studying interplanetary treaties, parsing tangled policies, and untangling subtle diplomatic feints gave him a quiet, decisive advantage. Where others hesitated, Kaelen advanced, each solution clicking into place like the tumblers of a lock.

He moved with calm precision, reading between the lines, anticipating traps buried within questions that seemed deceptively straightforward. His fingers traced the holographic prompt, not with arrogance, but with a measured certainty that this, finally, was a game he was born to play.

Surprisingly, Theron faltered. His usually unshakable focus fractured under the weight of riddles that defied linear strategy; frustration seeped in, visible in the tightening of his jaw and the restless dart of his eyes. The Neydrin's polished confidence cracked slightly, but enough for Kaelen to see the widening gulf between calculated preparation and true adaptability. This round belonged to the thinker, not the schemer.

When the final glyph dissolved into nothingness, silence reclaimed the chamber, thick and almost accusatory. Kaelen let out a breath he hadn't realized he was holding, feeling a flush of triumph tempered by the gnaw of fatigue. Around him, competitors emerged with expressions that betrayed everything from drained defeat to simmering resolve.

The respite was brief. Mechanical doors slid open with a resonant hum, beckoning them onward. Whatever bruised pride or mental strain lingered would have to wait. The next challenge was already coalescing, and the Games offered no mercy for hesitation.

The third challenge plunged them into a labyrinth of shimmering laser grids and shifting energy barriers, an electrified maze suspended over a chasm pulsing with erratic light. Every step demanded surgical precision; a single miscalculation meant a searing bolt of pain or instant disqualification. It was here that Kaelen fully grasped the quiet value of his tenuous alliance with Jax.

His breath caught in the dense, charged haze, his pulse thrumming hot beneath his skin as laser grids closed around him in a tightening cage. Panic clawed up his throat until his fingers found the small device Jax had slipped him aboard the Solaris. It seemed little more than a curiosity, a quiet promise that might never matter.

Now that he was hemmed in by slicing beams, he understood its worth in full. With desperation driving his movements, he thumbed it on. A subtle vibration rippled through the surrounding metal; the grid shivered, lines of light glitching for a fraction of a second, just long enough to slip through. To the spectators, it would look like sheer brilliance.

In truth, it was simply a quiet collaboration.

The maze demanded an intimate grasp of the arena's hidden workings; agility alone would never be enough. The barriers pulsed in irregular, stuttering patterns, driven by cryptic cycles and concealed triggers. Kaelen, nimble and relentlessly observant, charted a path through much of it by instinct, though each step remained slow and fraught with peril.

With every shifting phase, he pulled farther ahead, sidestepping the most lethal sequences through precise timing and subtle intervention. His rivals lagged, some hesitating at crucial junctures, others ensnared in arcs of searing light that left them staggering.

It was then that Kaelen grasped something deeper: alliances, however fragile, could be born not solely of strategy, but of trust. And in Jax, almost against expectation, he had found both.

The last phase was a merciless fusion of everything that had come before, a relentless onslaught of punishing terrain, hidden snares, and mental trials engineered to fracture even the strongest. It wasn't a single obstacle, but a cascading gauntlet: collapsing pathways, labyrinths that twisted and reformed, pressure-sensitive traps, riddles that siphoned time and clarity, and environmental shifts designed to erode nerves and orientation.

Exhaustion now hung over them all like a suffocating shroud. Every breath seared raw in Kaelen's chest; every muscle burned with spent effort. The psychological toll of unending peril pressed close, dark and heavy. One misstep meant elimination. One moment of hesitation, failure. Kaelen's thoughts had long since abandoned any notion of glory, politics, or legacy. Now there was only survival.

Adrenaline carried him where strength faltered. Strategy kept him steady when brute force failed. He remembered Jax's words: "Observe the terrain, sense the hum of the systems, read the patterns." That guidance, paired with their earlier collaboration, let Kaelen slip past hazards that others tried to batter their way through. Lyra shattered traps with sheer power; Khel muscled through collapsing tunnels with brute determination. Kaelen navigated unseen triggers, solved layered logic locks mid-sprint, and pivoted moments before chaos could swallow him.

His alliance with Jax, once a quiet convenience, had become his edge. He was neither the fastest nor the strongest. But in that final stretch, lungs raw, legs threatening collapse, Kaelen realized he had outlasted those who were. Not through defiance alone, but through thinking, adapting, enduring. The end lay just ahead. And he was still standing.

Throughout the ordeal, Kaelen maintained a deliberate detachment, navigating the chaos with an analyst's eye and a diplomat's quiet restraint. Every potential alliance was weighed with exact care. Lyra's relentless will impressed him, yet her utter ruthlessness gave him pause. Theron's brilliance was indisputable, but every word he uttered carried the subtle scent of hidden agendas. Beyond Jax, only Khel, with his calm strength and unvarnished honesty, offered a sliver of trust that felt unforced, even real.

Yet the greatest revelation came from within. Kaelen had endured. More than that, he had adapted. He had faced the brute demands of physical trials, the mental toll of constant intricate calculations, and the quiet treachery woven through shifting alliances. And he had not broken. Where once he had seen only his limitations, he now recognized a resilience forged in places he'd never thought to look.

As the survivors staggered toward the end chamber, medical drones swept silently overhead, tagging those who'd fallen behind for extraction. Their pale lights cut ghostly paths through the haze, and Kaelen felt the strange, sobering weight of being counted among the living.

The Gauntlet had not merely tested him; it had shaped him. This was no game, no spectacle to be consumed from afar. The Ascendance was a proving ground for leaders, for survivors, for something more elemental and unyielding. And though exhaustion clung to his bones and uncertainty lingered at the edges of every thought, Kaelen stepped forward, eyes sharpened, posture steadied.

The Gauntlet was only the beginning.

# CRACKS IN THE GAME

Even as the dust settled and congratulations rippled through the gleaming halls of Helios, something felt... wrong. There were too many eyes lingering a moment too long, too many hushed conversations that fell abruptly silent the instant Kaelen stepped into view. Voices dropped like stones in water, leaving only ripples of unease in their wake. He only caught fragments; "not supposed to be him" ... "shifted too early" ... "keep quiet"; before they dissolved into silence.

The polished floor seemed to tilt for half a heartbeat, a phantom echo of the Gauntlet's collapsing ledges. His balance returned, but the sense of unreality stayed. Applause echoed like static inside his head. Each burst of laughter or camera flash made his pulse jump as though another trap might spring open beneath his feet. His body hadn't yet learned the difference between danger and safety. Every instinct still braced for collapse, even here, beneath the shining glass ceilings of victory.

Helios glittered around him with orchestrated perfection: banners unfurling in artificial gravity, the scent of ozone and perfume mingling in the air, delegates smiling too widely for the cameras. Council envoys lingered near every viewport, their insignias catching the light like warning flares; symbols of power masquerading as pageantry. It was triumph dressed in ceremony, a victory staged with precision and polish.

But beneath the gold veneer, Kaelen felt the pulse of something colder; observation disguised as admiration. Even the corridor sensors seemed to pivot as he passed, their tiny red lenses pulsing like a heartbeat.

The Ascendance was a trial, yes, but he wondered if someone else had lit the fire... and for reasons none of them yet understood. His hand drifted to the small pouch of Earth soil at his belt, a quiet anchor against the gnawing suspicion that the ground beneath him was no longer steady.

The low hum of Helios had changed since the Gauntlet. It had become a softer pitch, almost like a breath drawn between words that followed him down every corridor.

At night, long after the crowds had dispersed and the ceremonial sheen of victory faded, Kaelen walked Helios's quiet upper halls alongside Khel.

The corridors hummed with faint energy flows; the glow of distant skylights diffused into something pale and sterile. Few words passed between them. They didn't need them. There was comfort in simply sharing the same heavy silence, two bodies bearing the same weary toll.

Kaelen remembered the moment in the Gauntlet when Khel had moved without hesitation to block a collapsing platform long enough for him to cross. That memory lingered as vividly as the burn in his lungs.

It was a long while before Khel broke the silence, his voice a low rumble. "Strength isn't always enough. You more than proved that."

Kaelen met his steady gaze but found no judgment there, only quiet respect. For a fleeting instant, Kaelen saw something almost fragile in the Jovian's expression: fatigue, or maybe doubt, hidden behind the stoicism of endurance.

"You weren't afraid?" Kaelen asked quietly.

Khel's mouth twitched in something that might have been a smile. "Only of failing someone else."

The admission was soft, almost lost beneath the hum of the station. As they parted ways outside their respective quarters, Kaelen lingered in the doorway for a moment, breathing in the recycled air that somehow felt sharper, more metallic than before.

The triumph of surviving the Gauntlet already felt distant, stripped of celebration and leaving him only with questions. He retreated into his room, the faint echo of footsteps trailing off behind him, a reminder that vigilance might soon matter more than strength.

The Gauntlet's shadow still clung to him in the days that followed, its rush of adrenaline and fatigue lingering like smoke in his lungs. He had survived, but the victory rang hollow, its edges sharp with doubt. It wasn't the bruises or the bone-deep exhaustion that troubled him. It was something else, something just beneath the surface.

At first, the signs were faint: a mis-routed message, a missing training log, a flickering security clearance. All easily dismissed as the noise of a vast interplanetary operation. Kaelen, however, wasn't buying it. He had grown up watching diplomats unravel entire nations with nothing more than a whisper. He knew the difference between chaos and intent. And this... felt intentional.

Each glitch he tested seemed to lead nowhere, like a trail deliberately scrubbed clean. With uncertainty all around him, the pouch at his side became the one piece of grounding reality he trusted. The soil felt heavier now, as though even Earth's gravity was trying to hold him in place.

He couldn't ignore the patterns forming behind these "accidents." The Committee's technology was far too precise for such sloppiness. So why the errors? Why now? The thought wormed deeper the longer he considered it. Maybe the Games were not failing; they were being manipulated. Controlled. Perhaps the system was bending toward someone's will. But whose? And to what purpose?

As the anomalies surfaced and multiplied, a darker thread wove itself through the fabric of the Games. He couldn't shake the feeling that something was unfolding behind the scenes. Kaelen suspected the Games were no longer about selecting a champion at all.

The first undeniable clue arrived during the second phase, the intellectual gauntlet. A logic puzzle, deceptively simple at first glance, relied on a sequence of interconnected symbols. On the surface, it seemed straightforward. But Kaelen caught the flaw: a subtle ambiguity rooted in archaic Martian glyphs.

Lyra, predictably, breezed through it. What drew Kaelen's attention, however, was Theron. The Neydrin strategist, brilliant and precise, a master of probability and abstract reasoning, hesitated and then faltered. Not for a lack of intellect, his mind was formidable. But the puzzle was designed to exploit exactly that strength, catching him in precisely the sort of nuance no genuine contest would exploit.

It was too elegant to be an oversight. It felt deliberate, a manipulation embedded in the rules themselves, giving one competitor an advantage while deftly undermining another. For the first time, Kaelen saw Theron's polished certainty splinter just for a heartbeat, and it unsettled him.

There were moments during the maze of shifting energy barriers when Kaelen witnessed something that he couldn't easily explain. Khel, the towering Jovian, came within a breath of triggering a lethal surge. Just as his hand hovered over the grid, the lasers flickered with an erratic stutter that pulled them out of reach at the last possible instant. It wasn't a random failure. It was too precise, too perfectly timed, as if something, or someone, had subtly intervened, shifting the barrier to spare Khel while maintaining the illusion of a harmless glitch.

Kaelen's pulse spiked, his hand brushing the soil pouch instinctively, grounding himself against the eerie sense that fate itself had been tampered with. This wasn't luck. It was control. And Kaelen glimpsed the outline of a game far more dangerous than the one they had been led to believe they were playing.

There were circumstances surrounding the sudden deaths of certain support staff during the trials that truly fueled Kaelen's suspicions. The first was a technician, found lifeless in his quarters, the official report calling it a heart attack. But Kaelen had seen him just that morning, laughing over coffee, vibrant with energy.

The second came days later: a medic discovered at the base of a towering platform, her spine shattered. They labeled it a tragic fall. Jax wasn't convinced. Quietly, he ran a private scan of the site, and what he uncovered chilled them both. Traced amounts of energy signatures unmistakably from a directed plasma weapon, the kind that didn't appear on any official inventory.

These weren't accidents. They were executions. Silent. Surgical. Intentional. Kaelen thought grimly of the cover stories his father once warned him about—always being too neat, too polished, designed to crumble under scrutiny. He encrypted Jax's findings under a diplomatic report title, disguising the data in harmless bureaucratic language. A habit learned from years of watching his father survive political crises through misdirection.

The cautious alliances he had once nurtured now strained and frayed under the weight of deepening suspicion. Lyra, who had at first been willing to trade brief words and strategies, withdrew behind a wall of dead silence, her gaze wary and distant, a reflection of the doubt Kaelen saw creeping into his own eyes. Her silence wasn't just caution; it was self-containment, as if she feared that words themselves could be overheard.

Theron remained utterly unreadable, his cool detachment betraying no concern, as if calculating that whatever conspiracy was unfolding might be sidestepped or quietly leveraged, but certainly not confronted. Only Khel, honest and steadfast, stayed close, offering a solid presence Kaelen could still lean on.

Yet even Khel's loyalty had limits; his understanding of the Ascendance stopped at the edge of brute trials and raw endurance. Beyond that, he was as much in the dark as anyone.

He wasn't completely alone. But the silence between allies sounded like the calm before something broke.

Outside his window, Helios drifted past the stars like a great, sleepless eye; unblinking... and waiting.

# A GAME WITHIN THE GAME

One evening, deep in Helios's diagnostic core, Kaelen stood over a frozen console, the telemetry glitching in patterns that no competent engineer would overlook. He was tracing the signal bleed, erratic spikes in the data stream that flickered and died like moths against a flame, when a voice broke the silence.

"Staring won't make the code rearrange itself."

He turned, mildly startled. Mira leaned in the doorway, her posture relaxed but her expression sharp, silver hair braided back tight. The pale light from the console cast hard angles across her face, giving her the look of someone carved from shadow and intent. Her tone held no sarcasm, just a dry practicality.

"You're tracking telemetry too?" he asked.

"I observe patterns," she replied. "This one's off. Timing inconsistencies, Phantom Echo channels. You're not imagining it."

"You think it's sabotage?"

"No," she said, stepping into the low light. "I think it's curated. Someone wants us to see just enough to grow suspicious, but not enough to act. Like a game within a game."

Kaelen frowned. "Why tell me?"

She met his eyes evenly. "Because I don't trust you. And I want to see what you do when the lights flicker and there's no one else watching."

Her gaze settled on the blinking console. "Whatever this is... it didn't start with us. And it won't end here."

With that, she walked away, her silence louder than any warning.

Kaelen remained frozen, staring at the data, her words echoing in his thoughts. Maybe he wasn't the only one pulling at threads, and maybe he'd just found a reluctant ally.

Of them all, only Jax continued to share what he uncovered. Mira had spoken her warning and vanished, her intent still unclear, but Jax's quiet loyalty became a rare constant amid growing uncertainty. But even Jax was just an engineer, not a spy; his genius thrived in circuitry and energy flows, not shadows and whispers. And Kaelen... Kaelen was beginning to understand that whatever was unfolding around them, they were painfully ill-equipped to stop it.

The Ascendance no longer resembled a contest of skill; it had been twisted into a battlefield artfully cloaked in spectacle. Somewhere behind all the pageantry, someone was pulling strings, shaping outcomes with a precision far too deliberate to be chance. The facade of fairness was cracking, revealing something far colder underneath.

His suspicion inevitably turned to the only entity with both the means and the motive: the Committee itself. Their omnipresence, once a source of order and reassurance, now felt menacing. They controlled the rules, the environment, even the very air the competitors breathed.

What had once seemed like impartial protocol now reeked of manipulation, their authority nothing more than a mask veiling something far more insidious. Paranoia pressed in on all sides; every shadow hinted at hidden threats; every hushed conversation crackled with the possibility of betrayal.

The other competitors, once mere rivals, now appeared as potential allies, though trust remained a scarce and fragile commodity. Kaelen knew he needed more than suspicions. He needed evidence, something concrete that would expose the truth before the rope drew any tighter.

One evening, while navigating the lesser-traveled maintenance corridors deep within Helios's inner complex, Kaelen noticed a faint seam on the wall, something so subtle most eyes would have just passed over. The panel was expertly camouflaged, nearly seamless, but a stray shaft of overhead light revealed a delicate shift in texture.

Driven by instinct and a rising pulse of curiosity, he worked it open and uncovered a single object tucked within the hollow chamber: an old data pad, still active, its interface locked beneath layers of encrypted firewalls. The smell of dust and oil clung to it, as though it had been hidden for years.

Uncertain of its contents but instinctively sensing its significance, Kaelen took the device straight to the only person he trusted to break its defenses; Jax. The Satori engineer accepted it without comment, disappearing into his private workshop like a ghost. Hours later he emerged, eyes shadowed, expression unreadable. "You need to see this," he said, his voice stripped of its usual calm.

What followed shattered everything Kaelen thought he knew. The data pad held detailed schematics of rigged challenges, records of covert sabotage, even logs implicating high-ranking Committee members in orchestrated assassinations.

The Ascendance wasn't simply manipulated; it was a controlled operation, a spectacle designed to mask something far darker. A coup engineered from the shadows. The Games, it would seem, had always been a lie.

Kaelen later found Mira standing alone in the hydroponics chamber, her back to the door, surrounded by the low hum of photosynthetic light panels and swaying strands of engineered algae. The recycled air was damp, heavy with the scent of chlorophyll and condensation. She didn't turn as he approached.

"You were right," he said simply.

"About what?" she asked, voice even, still facing the tanks.

"The glitches. The sabotage. The false trails. I saw them too. Jax decrypted something—"

"Stop." She finally turned, her gaze resembling a calm storm. "Don't say it here."

Kaelen hesitated. "Are you... already involved in something?"

Mira studied him. "I watch patterns. Patterns don't lie. People do."

He stepped closer. "If you have information..."

"I have questions," she interrupted. "And I prefer answers I uncover myself. Not those handed to me."

There was a long pause, the air between them heavy with both threat and possibility. Kaelen brushed his thumb over the soil pouch at his belt, grounding himself against the rising uncertainty.

"If I needed you," Kaelen asked quietly, "would you help?"

Mira didn't blink. "If I help you, it's because the answer benefits me too. Don't mistake alignment for allegiance."

Then she turned and walked away, leaving him amid the soft glow of artificial growth, wondering if he'd just gained an ally, or awakened a rival.

These files weren't just incriminating; they were damning.

Line by line, they revealed a chilling truth: the trials had never been fair. Some competitors had been marked for elimination long before they ever stepped into an arena. Others were sculpted for victory, their paths cleared by invisible hands. And presiding over it all was the Ascendance Committee, not impartial arbiters, but architects of a meticulous deception.

Their code names, signatures, and directives were all there, hidden beneath layers of encryption. The precise motives remained elusive, but the scale was unmistakable. This wasn't about the Games. It was about control. Domination. The quiet destabilization of entire worlds. And if left unchecked, it threatened not just planetary pride, but the unraveling of the solar system itself.

Kaelen's breath caught in his chest. The machine was already in motion, and now he was a threat to it. They would come for him next. Jax was the only one he could trust. The others were all brilliant and formidable, but untested in loyalty. Allies perhaps... or weapons that might turn on him without warning. He couldn't afford to guess wrong.

Going to the authorities was unthinkable. Too many channels were compromised. The Committee's reach was long, its eyes embedded in every corridor, every whispered report. Reaching Earth was out of the question. If Kaelen was going to act, it would have to be in silence, every move precise, invisible.

The days that followed blurred into a haze of encrypted messages, covert meetings, and shadows that lingered a heartbeat too long. Sleep became a stranger. Paranoia settled in as a necessary companion.

Eventually came the discovery that transmuted fear into raw dread: they weren't just manipulating the Ascendance; they were preparing to end it. Permanently. One final event. A manufactured catastrophe that would plunge Helios into chaos... and cement the Committee's hold over the system forever.

Desperation finally drove Kaelen to seek Lyra's counsel. He found her alone, sharpening her blades in a dim maintenance corridor, the walls pulsing with flickering fluorescent light. The sharp rasp of metal on stone filled the silence as sparks briefly lit her hardened face. She listened without interruption as he laid the decrypted files before her, evidence of sabotage, murder, and manipulation on a scale that stretched across worlds.

She didn't flinch. Didn't demand more proof. Instead, her eyes darkened with something harsher than surprise: recognition.

"I knew it," she murmured, voice low, edged with iron. "Not the whole picture. But I've seen the cracks. I've been following them."

Her own intelligence, gathered in the shadows, now aligned with Kaelen's. The threads interlocked. Together, they devised a desperate but necessary plan. The final challenge would no longer be fought simply in an arena; it would become their battlefield. Their reckoning. A trap sprung in reverse. They wouldn't just survive the Ascendance; they would tear away its illusions, drag its architects into the open, and force the truth screaming into the light.

The Ascendance had never been just a contest. It was the opening gambit in a much larger war... a war waged in the shadows.

# UNLIKELY BONDS

The weight of the conspiracy clung to Kaelen like smoke; inescapable, choking, and heavy with consequence. The revelation of a meticulously orchestrated coup had stripped away any last illusion that the Ascendance was a fair contest. It was no test of strength or intellect, but a purge. A quiet war draped in spectacle.

Even after uncovering the truth, Kaelen felt the machine around him still humming, indifferent and immense. Every corridor of Helios seemed to breathe now, the hum of its conduits no longer mechanical but predatory, as if the station itself were aware of what it was hiding. The light panels overhead flickered at odd intervals, and he caught himself wondering if it was surveillance or a warning.

The fragile alliances he once hoped might see him through began to fracture under the strain. Lyra, now a tentative partner in rebellion, still moved with the watchful precision of someone who trusted no one; her eyes betrayed nothing. Theron grew ever more distant, his sharp mind curling inward, consumed by self-preservation. Only Khel, the grizzled Jovian miner, remained steadfast; a silent pillar amid the rising storm, his loyalty unspoken and unwavering.

On a battlefield where trust was a rare currency and betrayal could strike within the next breath; Kaelen began to understand that survival would demand more than mere strength or cunning. It would hinge on knowing exactly where, and with whom, to place one's faith.

Khel, with his rough-hewn hands and quiet bearing, possessed a strength that went far beyond muscle. He spoke little, yet every movement carried a purpose that needed no explanation. Their bond, still new, still fragile, began to solidify during the subsequent trials: a grueling gauntlet of high-gravity obstacles, electrified platforms, and yawning voids beneath trembling ledges. Each element was meticulously designed not only to punish the body, but to strain the fragile trust between teammates.

Kaelen, still hampered by lingering injuries, fought to keep his footing on slick, energy-charged surfaces. Every muscle in his body screamed with fatigue, each breath rasping through the synthetic filtration of his lungs. The hum of the gravity field roared in his ears, disorienting and cruel. Sensing his struggle, Khel reached out without hesitation, his grip powerful and steady. With every step, every tentative shift of weight, he became a living anchor, guiding Kaelen through danger. He never spoke. He didn't have to. That quiet act of solidarity resonated louder than any vow could have.

Later that evening, in the dim silence of the competitor barracks, Kaelen took a seat beside Khel, their gear drying silently around them. The air smelled faintly of machine oil and rust. Helios never truly shed the scent of oiled machinery. No words passed at first; they didn't need them. The memory of the day's ordeal lived on in aching muscles and fresh bruises, and in the subtle nod Khel had given after pulling him across that final ledge.

For the first time in days, Kaelen felt something unfamiliar: trust. In this swirling vortex of deception and shifting allegiance, Khel's calm presence was like a fixed star in a spinning sky. It wouldn't last. Nothing in the Ascendance ever did. But for now, it was enough.

Khel's gaze remained steady, the kind that didn't demand answers but invited them. "Sometimes I think the real test isn't out there in the trials," he mumbled. "It's whether we can survive each other in here."

Kaelen offered a faint nod, unsure himself if it was agreement or resignation.

A door hissed open behind them.

"Touching," Lyra's voice cut through the moment like a scalpel. "Should we all hold hands and sing next?"

Kaelen glanced over his shoulder. "Only if you're leading the chorus."

She stepped forward, arms folded, not smiling. The low light caught the edge of her blade as she turned it absently in her hand; an act more habit than threat, but enough to shift the air.

"Don't mistake sentiment for strategy. If you want to survive the next trial, you'd better stop pretending this is about unity."

Khel rumbled, "Not everything has to be a battle."

"Spoken like someone who's never had to smile while someone plots your death." Her eyes brushed between them, sharp and unflinching. "I'm not here for your friendship. I'm here because none of us will make it alone."

Kaelen met her gaze. "Then maybe start acting like we're on the same side."

Lyra didn't blink. "I don't believe in taking sides. I believe only in the outcomes."

The words landed heavily, the kind that left silence in their wake. She turned and left, her boots striking the floor with a steady rhythm that lingered long after she was gone. The air felt colder in her absence.

Khel exhaled slowly. "I don't think she's wrong."

Kaelen nodded. "Neither do I, and that's what worries me."

Khel leaned back against the wall, arms crossed. "You trust her?"

Kaelen gave a tired half-smile. "I trust what she wants. For now, that's enough."

Khel grunted softly. "That's not trust. That's survival."

"Maybe that's all we have left," Kaelen murmured.

From the corridor's edge, Mira's voice drifted in, soft but cutting.

"You're wasting breath trying to change her mind. She only listens when she bleeds."

Kaelen raised an eyebrow. "And you?"

Mira's expression remained unreadable. "I listen when things stop making sense." Her gaze lingered a heartbeat longer than necessary before she vanished back into the corridor, leaving behind a faint echo of unease.

The first challenge of the next morning plunged them into the Gauntlet's submerged sectors, a flooded labyrinth buried deep within Helios's outer ring. The descent was silent and mechanical. Pressure doors sealed behind them one by one until the sound of the world above disappeared entirely.

Water closed in on all sides, cold and absolute. Light fractured into ghostly beams that cut through the gloom like a fading memory, and the weight of the depth pressed against Kaelen's chest until breathing felt like defiance.

The aim of this trial sounded simple: retrieve a coded relay from the lowest trench and return before oxygen reserves ran out. Execution, however, would prove to be anything but.

Kaelen's nano-gills activated beneath the skin of his neck in a faint, prickling cascade that drew oxygen directly from the water. It kept him alive, but every breath carried a strange metallic tang, leaving a subtle burn in his lungs as if his body refused to fully accept the process. He could hear his pulse thudding inside his skull, muffled and distorted, like the distant rhythm of war drums.

Visibility was abysmal. He could barely make out the murky outlines and the dim flare of distant beacons strapped to the other competitors. The water absorbed every sound; even his thoughts seemed to echo differently here, stretched thin by pressure. Panic edged closer with every blind turn, coiling around him like a predator as the tunnel twisted into a maze of false exits and groaning metal.

And then, out of the shifting haze, Khel appeared; silent, steady, a massive silhouette gliding through the blackness with impossible grace. Years spent mining beneath Jupiter's crushing mantle had shaped him into something more than human; he moved as if the depths were home. The faint bio-luminescence of his gills traced blue lines across his throat, ghostly and calm. When Kaelen's navigation system flickered out and his pulse surged into blind panic, Khel's hand found his arm without hesitation, his grip firm and grounding. I've got you. The words never needed to be spoken.

At a critical junction, Kaelen's vision started to blur with dark edges creeping inward as his nano-gills strained against the crushing depth. The water here was colder, starved of oxygen. His breaths came too fast. Disoriented and almost blind, he missed the half-buried relay wedged beneath a collapsed strut.

Khel was the one to spot it first. Without hesitation, he freed the device, pressed it into Kaelen's trembling hands, and gestured upward. The gesture was simple, but carried the weight of earned respect; yours to finish.

Kaelen kicked toward the surface, his lungs burning, muscles scream-ing, with the relay clutched tight against his chest. The current tugged like an unseen will trying to pull him back, but for the first time, something stronger than fear propelled him forward.

Those shared moments of quiet coordination under crushing pres-sure, life balanced on the edge of catastrophe, fractured the tempered shell of suspicion that had long encased Kaelen. In Khel, he didn't just see a competitor; he saw the possibility of genuine friendship.

Not the kind born of negotiation or necessity, but one forged in hardship and sustained by unspoken action. And Khel, for his part, seemed to sense Kaelen's quiet war against manipulation and dread, offering support without judgment or demand. What had begun as tactical cooperation was growing into something more rare than victory in these Games: trust.

One evening, beneath the muted glow of the Gauntlet's emergency lights, Kaelen and Khel sat together in a quiet alcove, trading stories of their home worlds. The hum of distant engines filled the silence between their words, a steady reminder that Helios was alive and listening.

Khel spoke first, painting vivid pictures of Jupiter's brutal beauty, a realm of colossal storms and crushing pressures where survival demanded unity as much as strength. He described mining colonies as fragile lanterns suspended in chaos, each life depending on the others to hold back oblivion. In that unforgiving world, brotherhood wasn't a virtue. It was survival.

Kaelen listened, the rhythm of Khel's voice grounding him more than he cared to admit. When his turn came, he spoke of Earth: of its delicate ecosystems and fractured history, of how diplomacy had been both humanity's salvation and its slow undoing.

For the first time, he felt he could share the truth of what he had uncovered: the decrypted files, the rigged trials, the assassinations, the looming catastrophe. The words spilled out like a confession, each one heavier than the last.

Khel listened in silence. His weathered face stayed unreadable, but in his eyes flickered something unmistakable: understanding. When Kaelen finished, there were no hollow reassurances, no easy words. Just the steady presence of someone who had seen the worst any world could offer and still stood on the side of what was right.

"They think they can control everything," Khel said at last, his voice low, like distant thunder. "But they forget... when you push people who've lost everything, they push back."

Kaelen looked up, meeting Khel's steady gaze. "You make it sound so simple."

"It is," Khel said. "Simple doesn't always mean easy."

Kaelen nodded slowly. "Then I suppose its time we remind them of what can't be controlled."

A faint smile ghosted across Khel's face. "Now you sound like someone worth following."

The words settled between them like a vow. Kaelen looked down at the small pouch of Earth soil tied to his belt, feeling its weight against his side. In that moment, he understood that resistance wasn't born from rage, but from recognition... from knowing that something within you refused to be owned.

For the first time since the Games began, Kaelen believed he might not be fighting alone.

# RECKONINGS

In the following days, resolve hardened into action. With Khel's quiet strength at his side, Kaelen threw himself into uncovering more. What had begun as a whispered conversation in the shadows quickly evolved into a coordinated effort, an underground resistance stitched together by fragments of truth and faint glimmers of hope.

Together, they dug deeper, combing through corrupted systems and encrypted logs, piecing together the scale of the conspiracy bit by bit. Every discovery felt like a small defiance against a machine designed to erase dissent before it could even form a thought.

At first, their allies were just reluctant technicians who glanced over their shoulders three times before slipping Kaelen fragments of corrupt telemetry. There were medics who pretended to change bandages while pressing encrypted drives into his palm, staff who had seen too much and spoken too little. Fear kept them cautious, but something in Kaelen's resolve, paired with Khel's immovable presence, drew them in.

One by one, the whispers turned into quiet offerings: passwords muttered under breath, back doors into surveillance blind spots, fragments of logs scrubbed hastily from official records. Every secret carried a risk, and every risk carried the weight of someone's life.

Helios itself seemed to bristle with warnings. Twice Kaelen stumbled upon maintenance crews running "emergency drills" that hadn't been announced by any official channels. Entire corridors were sealed without cause; oxygen reserves had been quietly rerouted, and evacuation paths were marked in chalk where no inspection teams were scheduled. The anomalies felt less like preparation and more like rehearsal; the quiet choreography of an ending none of the competitors were supposed to see.

The air itself carried a tautness, as if the station were holding its breath. Kaelen began to feel as though he was walking through the lungs of a living thing, one exhale away from collapse.

Their search eventually led them to a hidden alcove on the lower decks, where they sifted through encrypted caches under the cover of emergency lights. The metal walls throbbed faintly with power conduits like the pulse of the station's heart echoing through the floor.

It was here that Kaelen first noticed they weren't alone. Across the bay, Mira stood at the threshold of shadow, her silver hair catching the faint glow. She didn't speak or step closer; she only watched long enough to make Kaelen's skin prickle. Then she was gone, vanishing as if she had never been there at all.

The weight of their discoveries continued to mount until footsteps approached. Steps too light for Khel and too precise for Lyra. It was Aris who eventually stepped into the alcove, her arms crossed, with eyes glinting like polished glass.

She moved with the calm of someone who had lived too long in places where being overheard could mean death. The glow from Kaelen's interface carved her face in stark relief, every line sharpened into something predatory. She leaned against the wall, as if she owned the shadows themselves.

"You think you've cracked it, don't you?" she said, her voice measured and practiced. It carried a kind of cadence that didn't ask questions but laid traps. "You think you've found the big, ugly truth buried beneath all this spectacle."

Kaelen didn't look up. "I have."

"Good..." A flicker of amusement touched her mouth but never reached her eyes. "Then you'll understand why that truth doesn't matter."

He finally turned, brows furrowed. "What are you talking about?"

Aris tilted her head, with the faintest glint of contempt in her gaze. "It's not about what's real, Voss. It's about who controls the message. You could hand that truth to every system in the Belt, and it wouldn't change a thing unless someone in power decides it's useful."

"Then we change who's in power."

"You think this is a revolution?" she asked, her tone dropping to a whisper sharp enough to cut. "This is a media war. A war of perception... You want to fight it like a soldier. I fight it like a ghost."

Kaelen's jaw tightened. "So, you've known this whole time?"

"Longer than you have. But unlike you, I don't waste time chasing justice. I chase outcomes." She stepped closer, close enough that her shadow fell across his hands on the console. Her voice softened, becoming conspiratorial. "You want to win this? Stop trying to prove you're right and start being dangerous."

For a heartbeat, he saw her clearly; someone who had traded morality for survival and still carried the scars of that bargain.

Then, as suddenly as she had appeared, Aris was gone, leaving only the echo of her words and the fading hum of encrypted code.

Kaelen sat back, exhaling slowly. His hand brushed the soil pouch at his belt, grounding him against the razor edge of doubt. His father's voice came to him again, quiet but unrelenting: Control the board, not the pieces. That lesson, once meant for diplomacy, now bent itself into something far more dangerous. Aris's pragmatism had its allure (outcomes over ideals) but if he gave up justice entirely, how different would he be from the Committee itself? The question burned hotter than the fear he harbored.

Khel stepped out of the shadows, his expression unreadable. "She's not wrong," he said. "But she's not right either."

Kaelen looked up, exhaustion and determination warring behind his eyes. "Then what are we?"

Khel's gaze was steady and unflinching. "The ones who will never stop."

The scope of the revelation was staggering. Its implications weren't just planetary; they were galactic. Fear surged through Kaelen, sharp and immediate, but it didn't paralyze; it crystallized. The time for cautious observation had ended. He and Khel would have to act, and soon. Before the next move was made. Before the system tipped into irreversible darkness.

Armed with damning evidence and backed by a fragile network of quietly defiant allies, Kaelen and Khel would no longer be pawns in a rigged spectacle. They had a plan. Risky, audacious, and born of desperation, it was their only chance to drag the truth into the light.

Helios thrummed around them, a sleeping giant full of secrets. In the faint hum of its conduits, Kaelen thought he heard what could only be described as the rhythm of an awakening.

What began as a rivalry had transformed into a full-scale rebellion. And now the fate of entire worlds would hinge on strength, trust, resolve, and the unlikely alliance forged in the long shadow of betrayal.

The ultimate battle would no longer be about victory in the Games. It would be about saving everything.

# UNDERTOWS

The Neydrin were known across the Solar System for their intricately ruthless strategies and merciless precision, and none embodied that legacy more completely than Theron. He moved with the grace of a predator, each step deliberate, each glance heavy with silent calculation. While others relied on strength or forged visible alliances, Theron thrived in ambiguity, quietly pulling strings and shifting dynamics with a well-timed phrase or a subtle tilt of his head. His strategies mirrored the deep currents of Neptune itself: unseen, fluid and dangerously potent.

Kaelen watched all of this from a careful distance, tracking every understated maneuver, weighing Theron's veiled tactics against his own rising resolve. In a competition where brute force drew the headlines, Theron played the long game. He remained unseen, unspoken, and always three moves ahead.

Kaelen knew better than to underestimate the quiet power of a man who preferred to work in the shadows.

Although initially wary of Theron's enigmatic nature, he soon found himself drawn into an unspoken game of intellect and anticipation. He watched the Neydrin with growing fascination, noting how he navigated each challenge without brute force, using razor-sharp foresight instead.

In one trial, a collaborative puzzle demanding split-second coordination, Theron seemed to glide through chaos, effortlessly predicting his opponents' moves before they made them. His genius wasn't in overpowering the competition, but in quietly manipulating its very architecture, bending the rules without ever breaking them. He crafted diversions, nudged rivals toward false leads, exploited their assumptions, all while maintaining an air of detached calm. It wasn't cheating, at least not overtly. It was something just as dangerous: a masterclass in control.

During a high-stakes negotiation over resource distribution aboard a simulated space station, Theron's brilliance shone with chilling clarity. While others argued passionately, driven by pride, desperation, or raw ego, Theron remained silent, his expression unreadable. He cataloged every outburst, every weakness, every subtle tell. Then, at the exact moment when tensions threatened to spill over, he spoke. Not loudly. Not forcefully. But with surgical precision.

His proposals, although always framed as reasonable compromises, subtly fractured alliances, stoked insecurities, and redirected ambitions. By the time the dust settled, Theron had secured the lion's share of the resources without ever appearing to grasp for power. It was manipulation elevated to an art form, psychological warfare that needed no weapons.

Kaelen quietly weighed Theron's cold calculations against his own hardening resolve. It was a sobering lesson: in a contest like this, victory didn't always belong to the strongest, or even the cleverest. Sometimes it went to the one willing to pull the most invisible strings.

Both fascinated and slightly unsettled by Theron's quiet mastery, Kaelen studied him with growing focus. He noted the subtle shifts in posture, the fractional pauses before a response, the nearly impercep-tible inflections that hinted at deeper intentions.

It was evident Theron's actual strength lay in his uncanny ability to read people, parsing motivations, detecting vulnerabilities, anticipating reactions before they fully formed. The smallest flicker of doubt or the slightest tremor in someone's voice could become a tool in Theron's hands. A lever he could use to steer conversations and manipulate entire outcomes without ever having to touch them.

One evening, Kaelen found himself alone with Theron on the observation deck, overlooking simulated stars that shimmered like distant, half-kept truths. The faint hum of environmental stabilizers filled the silence like a second heartbeat. He began with casual talk of the next challenge, but his real aim was subtler: to peel back the layers of Theron's methods.

Theron, of course, offered nothing directly. Instead, he spoke in oblique parables of shifting tides and silent currents, of patient predators and the blindness of prey. Each story was a lesson wrapped in metaphor, a glimpse of the strategy beneath his calm exterior. Kaelen listened intently, parsing every word for hidden meaning, aware that even this conversation was likely another calculated move in a game only Theron fully understood.

"Power," Theron murmured at last, his voice barely rising over the gentle hum of the deck, "is not brute force. It's knowing the currents and when to ride the wave."

He paused; eyes fixed on the glittering void beyond the glass. "The sharpest blade is still just steel. But the mind... the mind reshapes the battlefield before a single move is made."

Then he turned his gaze to lock with Kaelen's, an unreadable expression on his face. "In any contest of strategy, the most dangerous player is the one who seems least so. The quiet one. The observer. The one who listens while others reveal their weaknesses."

As Theron's words sank in, Kaelen began to grasp the strategist's true strength. It wasn't force or overt command. It was invisibility, the power to remain unnoticed while subtly steering the course of events. Theron didn't challenge the system; he bent it from within, exploiting every flaw that others overlooked. A master of indirect influence, shaping outcomes through precision and patience, always three moves ahead.

When Theron left, Kaelen lingered at the viewport, his reflection ghosted against the stars. For the first time, he wondered if learning from a man like Theron meant becoming one. The thought left a faint chill throughout his body. There was brilliance in manipulation, but also corruption in its mastery.

He incorporated Theron's techniques into his own approach. He listened more intently, watched with sharper eyes, and learned to anticipate his opponents' moves before they made them. Subtlety became his weapon: an arched eyebrow here, a precisely timed silence there, the careful art of suggestion over force. Bit by bit, he started shaping outcomes, tilting the odds in his favor without ever appearing to. And in doing so, he uncovered the invisible threads of power that bound every action, every decision within the Games.

One trial placed them at the heart of a complex political simulation, negotiating alliances and resolving tensions within a fabricated inter-stellar council. Drawing on what he'd gleaned from Theron, Kaelen approached it with measured restraint. He positioned himself as a neutral voice of reason, allowing others to speak first, observing the fractures in their unity.

When the moment was right, he offered carefully crafted remarks, never forceful, always timely, that nudged factions toward either division or cohesion, whichever best served his aims. He even aligned with opposing sides at different intervals, subtly shifting loyalties without ever forfeiting trust. By the scenario's end, he stood unscathed and quietly in control, earning not only a critical advantage in the com-petition, but a new respect from those who had once underestimated him.

His improved strategic thinking and his adoption of Theron's understated manipulations soon translated into decisive victories across subsequent challenges. Repeatedly, he outmaneuvered rivals with foresight and precision, learning to read the faint cues of hesitation, the tells of desperation or pride, predicting movements before they happened. Weaknesses became windows; flaws turned into footholds. He bent the rules artfully, never breaking them outright, exploiting angles others overlooked.

With each triumph, Kaelen's confidence grew alongside a sobering clarity. The real contest wasn't simply winning here. It was preparation for the battles that waited beyond Helios, in the shadowed corridors where power truly shaped the fate of worlds.

Yet each victory came with a whisper of unease. His reflections grew longer at night, staring into the sterile light of his quarters, asking whether cleverness and control were simply the Committee's tools dressed in new hands. Was he learning to dismantle manipulation... or to wield it?

As he studied Theron more closely, he could see a pattern, not of cold amorality, but of stark necessity. Theron never moved without purpose; every quiet ploy was anchored to survival within a system steeped in deception. Slowly, Kaelen came to understand that in this arena, integrity wasn't about staying clean. It was about knowing when to get dirty and for what cause.

The air in the debriefing chamber crackled with restrained hostility. Lyra paced near the data wall, arms folded tight, her jaw set like a locked vault. Aris leaned against the opposite bulkhead, flicking a small magnet between her fingers, expression unreadable but loaded. Between them, tension swirled; old wounds, newer suspicions, unspoken contempt began to fill the room.

Selene stood between them, calm and motionless. Her hands were clasped loosely behind her back; her voice was quiet but unshakable. "You're both circling the same point," she said. "Just from opposite ends."

Lyra stopped pacing. "Don't be condescending."

"I'm not," Selene said evenly. "But if you keep letting your pride dictate your strategy, you'll both lose."

Aris smirked, though it didn't reach her eyes. "And you're here to save us, is that it?"

Selene turned, her gaze steady. "I'm here because if we splinter now, we hand them exactly what they want. Infighting is the first symptom of a dying resistance."

Lyra scoffed. "Don't talk to me about resistance. I've bled for this."

"So have we all," Selene replied. "The difference is, I know how to keep that blood from becoming a spectacle."

Aris pushed off the wall. "Then what do you suggest, diplomat?"

Selene stepped forward, her voice low but sharp. "You both want control. Fine. Keep your factions. Keep your tempers. But when it matters, when the real move comes, you'll listen. Because unlike either of you, I know how to make people believe what they fear. And I know how to make them act on it."

The room fell into a brittle silence...

Lyra, after a long pause, offered the slightest of nods. Aris didn't speak, but she stood firm in her gaze of the group.

Selene turned to leave. "We don't have to like each other. But we will act in concert. Or we won't act at all."

Kaelen had watched the exchange from a distance, saying nothing. He didn't need to. Selene had wielded the moment like a scalpel, no raised voice, no show of strength, just perfectly calibrated restraint. Where Theron used shadows and silence, Selene used poise and pressure. Two masters of influence, sculpting outcomes with opposite tools. And somewhere between them, Kaelen realized, lay the path he'd have to walk: one eye on principle, the other on survival.

As the final challenge loomed, Kaelen felt both sharpened and scared.

He was more prepared than ever but knew the coming war would blur the lines between ally and adversary, right and wrong, until they were all but indistinguishable. The real test would not simply be survival. It would be what remained of him afterward.

And just as Kaelen grasped the dangerous sophistication of the games-manship swirling around him, a new variable entered the equation. It was quiet, brilliant, and impossible to ignore. Something, or someone, had begun watching from the edges of every data stream, intercepting his signals, mimicking his encryption keys. The hunter was no longer unseen.

The next move would not belong to him.

# FRACTURED LOYALTIES

The atmosphere was electric with tension, charged by suspicion and the bitter scent of betrayal. Fragile illusions of unity shattered, leaving only wary glances and unspoken accusations hanging in the air. The chamber itself seemed complicit, its recycled air heavy, the hum of machinery now a mocking whisper.

Every shadow stretched longer; every silence felt deliberate, as if the station itself were holding its breath, waiting for someone to make the first mistake.

Khel was the first to voice what everyone already felt. The Jovian pragmatist, usually gruff but dependable, now carried a sharper edge.

"Something's off," he muttered, his eyes sweeping over the gathered competitors like a commander scanning a battlefield for ambush.

His words sliced through the silence like a miner's drill striking stone. "Feels like we're being played."

The statement struck a chord deep within them. Seeds of doubt began to take root, coiling tighter with each breath. The alliance, once solidified by shared peril and hard-won trust, fractured under the weight of suspicion. Whispers became wary glances that developed into sharp words, then edged into quiet accusations.

The air thickened with mistrust, every conversation shadowed by the lurking possibility of betrayal. Even the walls felt closer, as though Helios itself fed on their doubt, amplifying every flicker of tension into a storm.

Accusations flew like daggers, sharper and more venomous with each exchange. Kaelen found himself ensnared in a web of lies and half-truths, unable to truly tell ally from adversary. Alone in the heart of this psychological labyrinth, he stood as the last fragile thread holding their coalition together, though he wasn't sure how much longer the thread could bear the weight.

Suspicion coalesced around Jax. His quiet competence, once a source of reassurance, now seemed disturbingly methodical. The very talents that had made him indispensable, his seamless access to secure networks, his uncanny knack for disabling critical systems—suddenly appeared damning. Had he been playing both sides from the start?

Kaelen's thoughts spun back through every cryptic comment, every inscrutable look. In hindsight, Jax's musings on power, control, and necessity sounded less like observations and more like quiet confessions.

Lyra, her tightly wound composure beginning to crack, gave a slow, deliberate nod. "Too many coincidences. Too many threads being pulled at exactly the right moments," she said, her voice low, tense. Then her gaze flicked to Theron, who stood slightly apart, arms crossed, face carved into something unreadable. His silence, once a pillar of stoic reassurance, now seemed ominous and heavy with implication.

A chill traced down Kaelen's spine. Theron wasn't just being quiet. He was withholding something.

Seeking to refocus the group, Theron pivoted, outlining a meticulous approach for the upcoming hazard course. His tone was cold, an icy blade cutting through the room's uneasy quiet.

Nearby, Jax leaned against a console, an inscrutable grin playing at his lips. "Or..." he said, "we bypass three-quarters of that with a short-range pulse disruptor. Assuming you're not afraid of voiding a few safety protocols."

The room fell silent. Theron's eyes hardened, a quiet challenge thrown. Kaelen took it all in, unsettled by how quickly the lines had blurred.

Aris, who had been silent until now, stepped forward from the shadows with a look of thinly veiled disdain.

"You're both operating like this is still a controlled simulation," she said sharply.

"But we're on a battlefield laced with variables you can't predict, and leadership through ambiguity is going to get us all killed."

Jax straightened from where he leaned, brow arching. "You have a better plan, Aris?"

"I have a better objection," she snapped.

"We can't just follow Theron's strategy because it sounds precise. And we can't keep playing wildcard to your next hack job, Jax. Both of you treat us like pawns to maneuver, not equals."

Theron's eyes narrowed, but he said nothing. The silence that followed was colder than contempt.

Aris pressed on, her voice rising. "We need a tactical council, not a hierarchy hidden behind charisma and shadows. One vote per head, no secret sub-channels, no unilateral moves. You want us to trust you?"

She looked between them. "Then stop acting like tyrants cloaked in strategy."

For a heartbeat, no one moved. Then Kaelen nodded slightly. "She's right."

Lyra murmured, "Finally, someone said it."

Mira stepped forward quietly, her voice lacking Aris's heat but carrying something else; tired conviction.

"I didn't survive the Satori archives just to watch us destroy each other now," she said, looking not at Jax or Theron, but at Kaelen and Lyra.

"We've all fought different wars, but we're here because we saw something worth saving. Maybe we're fractured, but so is the system. If we don't figure out how to hold this line together, there won't be another one."

Her eyes lingered on Lyra for a breath. Just long enough to acknowledge something unspoken between them: the shared weight of impossible expectations. Then she stepped back, the moment gone, but its gravity remained.

The air shifted, charged with a brittle stillness. Deep within the station, a vibration trembled through the deck plating. It radiated like a low, metallic pulse that echoed a heartbeat. Kaelen couldn't tell whether it came from the machinery or from the collective tension winding tighter by the second.

Jax struck first. With a scowl etched deep across his forehead, he leveled a direct accusation at Theron, presenting a trove of encrypted messages that hinted at covert communications between the strategist and high-ranking Satori officials. He also produced records of concealed digital transactions, suggesting a hefty payoff.

The evidence was circumstantial, but in the charged atmosphere of mistrust, it was more than enough to plant the seeds of profound doubt.

At last, Theron broke his silence. His confession hit like a shot in the dark.

His words were almost clinical as he admitted partial involvement with the agents of the conspiracy. Not a core conspirator, he claimed, but a desperate pawn in a game he'd never fully controlled.

He revealed his motives to be rooted in a fierce, unspoken loyalty to Neptune; an embattled world slowly strangled by Saturn's calculated "diplomatic progress."

His voice remained low but unwavering as he laid out his defense, one that was either meticulous truth or masterful deception. He hadn't betrayed them, he claimed; he had played the role of collaborator to infiltrate the conspirators' inner circle, positioning himself to sabotage their plans from within.

The payments? Compensation for carefully crafted disinformation designed to cripple the conspiracy's operations. His silence, he argued, was the cost of sustaining the illusion. He had risked everything, not for personal gain, but to dismantle their enemies from the inside out.

Theron had entered the Competition hoping to expose Saturn's infringement, but blackmail, threats, and relentless coercion had forced him into silence. Now, he insisted, he was free from their grasp and ready to make amends.

His explanation, though plausible, left a residue of unease that refused to dissipate. It was a story impossible to verify, or to fully dismiss, not with the precious little time they had left.

Truth itself had become a labyrinth, each path twisting deeper into uncertainty. The air between them thickened with suspicion; every glance was a silent accusation, every pause a fresh wound cut by doubt. The fragile trust that had once bound their alliance lay shattered, and now even the most familiar faces seemed cloaked in quiet menace.

Kaelen watched Theron closely, parsing every word, every flicker of expression, trying to reconcile this confession with the icy strategist he'd come to both respect and fear. Theron's calm delivery didn't falter once, and that, more than anything, unnerved him.

The revelation cracked open a Pandora's box of suspicion. Trust, once fragile but functional, splintered under its weight. If Theron had once served the conspirators, even under duress, who else might hide fractured loyalty? The line between ally and enemy had grown so faint it was nearly meaningless.

For Kaelen, a diplomat's son trained to navigate conflict through clarity and reason, the moral fog was suffocating. He no longer knew whom to trust, or whether trust even mattered anymore. Every word, every gesture, every act of cooperation now demanded proof. Proof in Helios, however, was a commodity that came with a hefty price.

The weight of the Solar System's fate pressed down on Kaelen's shoulders, an invisible burden far heavier than any physical trial he'd ever endured. He was no longer just a competitor; he had become a reluctant leader, forced to navigate a maze of human fear, deception, and fractured loyalties.

The path ahead would be shadowed and treacherous; the line between friend and foe smeared into obscurity. This final showdown would not be a contest; it would be a desperate gamble for survival.

Yet, amid the ruins of trust, a flicker of resolve endured. Kaelen's hand brushed the soil pouch at his belt. The world beyond Helios felt impossibly far, but that fragment of Earth reminded him of who he was and why he endured.

He drew a slow breath, forcing steadiness into lungs that wanted to tremble. To him, the survival of the Solar System hinged on one thing: the courage to trust his instincts, even when every scrap of logic and evidence urged otherwise. The way forward was murky, but hesitation was no longer an option.

He had to act... and soon.

# SABOTAGE

The Satori representative, Jax Petrova, was a marvel of engineering prowess. His reputation preceded him; quietly acknowledged throughout the Ascendance as one of those rare minds that moved with breathtaking speed and elegant simplicity.

From the earliest challenges, Jax had distinguished himself, offering not just his help, but innovations that subtly, yet decisively, shifted the balance of power in Kaelen's favor.

His composure stood in stark contrast to the volatility of the other competitors, a point of stillness amid the surrounding storm. In Jax, Kaelen found not only technical mastery but an almost unnerving clarity. He was an enigma of efficiency, so precise he seemed less a rival than the silent linchpin of something far larger.

In the early days, Jax had seemed like a lifeline. Where the corridors of Helios felt suffocating, Jax brought clarity. During one trial, Kaelen recalled, he had been drowning in cascading readouts, warnings spilling across his visor faster than he could parse them. Jax had simply leaned over, tapped a sequence of commands, and explained in calm, clipped words, "Ignore the noise. Follow the core signal." The problem had dissolved, and Kaelen had felt, for the first time, like maybe he wasn't alone in these Games.

Drawn first by that quiet steadiness, Kaelen found himself increasingly reliant on Jax's insight. His sharp analysis cut through the swirl of uncertainties that clouded each new trial. Kaelen sought his counsel often, not just on technical obstacles, but for perspective in a competition where every decision carried hidden consequences.

Unlike Theron, who maneuvered from the shadows, Jax operated entirely in the open. His brilliance was unassuming yet undeniable. Where Theron sowed ambiguity, Jax offered direction. His presence became a fixed point, a stabilizing influence that Kaelen clung to amid gathering doubts.

Yet beneath Jax's composed, collaborative exterior ran a deeper current, an ambition that quietly diverged from his public persona. His loyalty to Saturn, while genuine, was not absolute. It was tempered by a private mission: to eclipse even the most celebrated engineers of his world and carve his name indelibly into the annals of scientific achievement. This drive wasn't born of malice, but of an unshakable certainty in his own brilliance.

To Jax, the Ascendance was never merely a competition. It was a proving ground, a stage upon which his genius could no longer be ignored. Kaelen observed in his quiet way, weighing each subtle shift against the measure of his own growing resolve.

That hidden ambition revealed itself in delicate, almost artful ways. During their collaboration, Jax consistently nudged strategies toward solutions that, while effective, also spotlighted his ingenuity. His suggestions seemed altruistic and quick, clever insights offered without ego, but a closer look revealed the precise choreography of a calculated performance.

Each innovation didn't just solve a problem; it burnished Jax's legend. More troubling still was his uncanny knack for anticipating upcoming challenges. It was too sharp, too tailored, as if fed by some clandestine source whispering from behind the curtain.

Slowly, an uneasy realization gnawed at the very fiber of Kaelen's being. What once seemed like quiet confidence now carried a faint metallic tang of manipulation. He started catching the small tells: the fractional pauses before Jax spoke, the careful positioning in every briefing, always where credit might naturally fall.

His insights remained razor sharp, his support unwavering, but beneath it pulsed a self-interest that grew harder to ignore. Doubt seeped in. Was Jax truly an ally, or a strategist cloaked in cooperation, using him, and the entire competition, as a stage for his own ascent? The more Kaelen questioned, the clearer it became that he was walking a tightrope strung dangerously between trust and betrayal.

One evening, during a tense challenge involving the repair of a damaged spacecraft, Jax's duplicity veered dangerously close to exposure. The environment simulation had glitched mid-trial, throwing them into a chaos of alarms and flashing crimson light. A critical component had vanished, and without it, the entire system teetered on the brink of catastrophic failure. Panic ripped through the competitors as precious seconds bled away.

The spacecraft's alarms screamed in shrill waves, the chamber trembling as sparks rained from exposed conduits. The acrid stench of burning metal stung Kaelen's nostrils as he scrambled to stabilize the failing reactor line. His hands shook as he fumbled with a half-melted coupling. Beside him, Jax's voice remained maddeningly calm, his tone even as though they were solving a puzzle at leisure.

"Rotate the stabilizer. Thirty-two degrees clockwise. Now hold."

His steadiness should have been an anchor, but instead, it chilled Kaelen to the bone. No one stayed that calm unless they knew the outcome beforehand.

It wasn't the calm of confidence, but of certainty. He knew exactly where the missing part was.

As he guided Kaelen through the frantic repair, Jax embedded a subtle modification, a change so minor it would evade any immediate scrutiny and dramatically boost the craft's performance. On the surface, it looked like a stroke of inspired genius, a last-minute save that would once again polish Jax's legend. But Kaelen saw through the deception. This wasn't brilliance born of pressure. It was manipulation cloaked in competence. And it left him cold.

For the rest of the trial, Jax worked with surgical focus, voice low, expression unreadable. When the alarms finally died and the lights steadied, the spectators erupted in praise. Cameras swiveled toward Jax; the Committee's feeds splashed his name in glowing fonts. But Kaelen barely heard them.

Beneath the applause, he felt only the low hum of the ship and the sudden hollowness between them, their mutual trust, severed cleanly.

Later that night, the barracks were quiet. Kaelen sat in the dim glow of his bunk lamp, his soil pouch warm in his palm. The recycled air hummed faintly with distant machinery. He thought of his mother's words of resolve and strength, and for the first time felt the sting of failure... not in defeat, but in misplaced trust.

Had he blinded himself out of necessity, seeing in Jax not who he truly was, but who he wanted him to be? The thought coiled deep, leaving Kaelen unsettled, even frightened; not of Jax, but of himself. If he could not tell ally from rival, how long before he betrayed his own instincts?

The realization struck Kaelen like a splinter beneath the skin. It was small, but impossible to ignore. From that moment on, he scrutinized Jax's every move, parsing each well-timed suggestion for hidden angles. Guidance that had once offered clarity now felt like a veiled trap. He found himself second-guessing, hesitating, wary of deceptions that might not even exist.

The synergy they once shared unraveled into strained silences and clipped exchanges, their once-seamless collaboration transformed into a quiet battlefield. Even in moments of calm, Kaelen couldn't shake the sense that he was still a piece on Jax's board, not moving by his own volition, but by the unseen hand of someone playing a far more personal game.

The growing distrust between them took a visible toll. In the next series of challenges, what had once been seamless coordination gave way to hesitation and second-guessing.

Kaelen, wary of falling under Jax's subtle influence, edged his input aside. Delicately at first, but not long before it turned into unmistakable caution.

Jax's innovative suggestions, often the best path forward, were met with guarded skepticism or bypassed outright. Kaelen told himself it was prudence, a necessary safeguard. But deep down, he recognized it for what it truly was: mistrust taking root in the cracks that necessity had left behind.

The impact was immediate. Their performance didn't collapse, but the keen edge that had once set them apart became noticeably dull. Other teams surged ahead, capitalizing on openings that Kaelen and Jax might once have closed with a glance. Tasks that should have flowed with intuitive precision now stuttered under the weight of silent caution. The partnership that had felt elemental, almost effortless, calcified into a cold standoff, a quiet tug-of-war strung beneath every clipped reply and guarded look.

Sometimes, Kaelen caught a flicker of hurt in Jax's eyes when his advice was dismissed, a flash of something human, fragile even. But it had vanished as quickly as it had come, replaced by his habitual mask of composure. The silence that stretched between them wasn't born of strategy anymore. It was heavier, more punishing than any argument between them. It was an unspoken acknowledgment of lost trust, and perhaps irretrievably so.

This internal struggle between Kaelen and Jax echoed a broader, more insidious conflict brewing within the Competition itself. The shadows cast by the growing conspiracy lengthened daily, infecting every interaction with a creeping suspicion. Trust wasn't only eroding between individuals; it was unraveling across the entire fabric of the Ascendance.

Allies eyed one another with quiet calculation, and motives that once seemed noble now appeared dangerously opaque. Jax's subtle manipulations were no longer just personal betrayals; they stood as symptoms of a deeper rot, reflections of the systemic deceit festering at the heart of these Games.

The spacecraft repair incident marked a pivotal shift, not only in how Kaelen viewed Jax, but in his understanding of the Competition itself. He saw that the true contest ran deeper than physical endurance or intellectual cunning. This was a war of ambition, where personal triumph was often paid for in the currency of trust.

Jax's maneuver cemented a darker truth: loyalty here was fluid, molded by opportunity far more than by principle. From that point on, Kaelen recognized the Ascendance for what it truly was, a ruthless political theater where every alliance carried a hidden cost.

As the Games progressed, Kaelen grew increasingly isolated, caught between the faint embers of trust and the cold weight of suspicion. Even those he had once considered closest, Jax chief among them, could no longer be seen without a shadow of doubt. The veneer of camaraderie had fractured, revealing the brutal calculus of power and legacy beneath.

It was a sobering revelation, but one that brought its own grim clarity. He understood now that success in this arena would demand more than intellect or technological finesse; it would require a strategist's foresight and a diplomat's subtlety.

The conspiracy still loomed, dark and patient at the margins of every challenge, and Kaelen knew that the final confrontation would test more than skill; it would probe his ability to navigate the fragile, perilous web of human allegiance.

The Satori's sabotage had left him with a bitter understanding:

in these Games, trust was the rarest currency of all... and the most dangerous to spend.

For the first time since Helios's golden halls had swallowed them whole, Kaelen truly felt alone. And somewhere in that isolation, a resolve began to take shape, not to survive, but to expose what the Games had become, even if it meant burning every bridge left standing.

Across the barracks, in the thin blue glow of a dormant console, Jax sat by himself. The data streams he had once found symphonic now droned like static. He replayed the moment Kaelen had turned away, the subtle shift of tone, the doubt that had replaced trust. He told himself it didn't matter, that outcomes outweighed sentiment, that this was simply the price of clarity.

Yet when he looked down at his hands, steady, precise, capable of saving or sabotaging lives with the same motion, he felt the faint tremor of something unfamiliar. Not guilt. Not yet. Something quieter: the creeping awareness that, in mastering control, he might have lost the one person who still saw him as more than the machine he had made himself to be.

The console's light flickered out. Shadows closed in, swallowing the last trace of warmth.

Jax sat alone in the silence until even the low hum of Helios faded away.

# REDBORN'S SECRET

On the horizon, the last challenge still loomed: a labyrinthine simulation of a collapsing asteroid field, engineered to push competitors to their absolute limits, demanding split-second decisions and unbreakable coordination. Yet Kaelen's unease had little to do with the overwhelming threat of the arena. It was something deeper, more insidious.

The conspiracy still writhed beneath the surface, coiling tighter by the hour, and time was running out. His alliance with Khel held firm, a rare constant amid shifting loyalties. But Lyra's silence had gotten to him. She stayed distant, her movements precise, her eyes cold and impossible to read.

Theron, ever the portrait of detached calculation, betrayed nothing, except for one nearly imperceptible shift in posture when Lyra entered the room. It was slight, but to Kaelen it rang like a warning bell. Something was wrong. And the answer, he realized, might not lie with Theron at all, but with the Redborn.

Lyra, a veteran of countless simulated wars, had remained an enigma throughout the Ascendance. Her skills were beyond question: every action surgically precise, every decision stripped of hesitation. At first, Kaelen wrote off her detachment as the Martian way, discipline over emotion, victory carved from vulnerability's corpse. But during a rare lull between challenges, something changed. He caught a flicker behind her otherwise flawless composure, a fleeting stutter of the eyes that reminded him of a system glitching under strain. It wasn't a weakness. It was something else. Something buried so deep it barely dared to surface.

Kaelen's instincts, honed through every subtle betrayal and hard lesson of these Games, tightened around that fragile thread.

That night, beneath the pale wash of the arena's artificial moonlight, Kaelen found Lyra sitting alone, silhouetted against the simulated star field. She sat with a rigid posture. Like a monument carved from Martian stone; unyielding. Kaelen approached cautiously, each step deliberately paced, his pulse thrummed hard in his chest.

He didn't confront her outright. Instead, he began quietly, with idle thoughts about the final challenge, the brutal unpredictability of the asteroid simulation, the weight pressing on them all. Then, carefully, he steered the conversation toward Earth, speaking of its fragile ecosystems, its long history of violence tempered by rare flashes of unity.

His words floated between them like offerings, probing for a crack in her formidable armor, a glimpse of the woman hidden behind the relentless warrior.

Slowly, Lyra answered. Her voice was low, almost reluctant, stripped of the clipped authority she wore so easily on the training grounds. She didn't recite Martian supremacy or boast of ancient triumphs; instead, she spoke of deep scars scorched into red soil and memory.

Mars, she admitted, hadn't been spared the wrath of the stars. Decades ago, a solar flare of unprecedented magnitude tore through the planet, crippling infrastructure and reducing cities to ash. Official histories praised glorious resilience and tactical retreat.

But Lyra offered the truth: chaos, despair and the quiet collapse of a civilization that had once dared to rival Earth. She had been but a child then, pulled from the smoldering ruins and reformed into something

93

harder than steel. Not raised but engineered. Trained not just to fight, but to win at any cost.

For Mars, the Games were never about honor; they were about survival, raw and brutal, a stage on which to prove to the Council that Mars still had value, still deserved a place at the table. Her silence, her cold detachment, Kaelen realized, wasn't arrogance. It was armor, hammered into place by necessity.

Her revelations came one after another and shattered everything Kaelen thought he knew. The solar flare, Lyra confided, hadn't been a natural disaster. It was a carefully orchestrated sabotage, an engineered catastrophe coordinated by a rogue faction within the Sol Federation. Its aim: to cripple Mars, eliminate a rival, consolidate power through systematic devastation. The flare's trajectory had been deliberate, guided to scorch the surface and plunge an entire world into ruin.

Lyra, having lived through it, watched her city vanish beneath waves of searing plasma. She had listened to the death throes of a planet betrayed by its kin. What remained of her people fled underground, fractured and desperate. The official narrative still sang of Martian fortitude, but for Lyra, the Ascendance was no quest for prestige. It was a last grasp at survival, a desperate bid to secure resources and alliances so Mars might breathe another century. Every match she fought, every enemy she outmaneuvered, was one more heartbeat for a civilization on the brink of extinction.

And in that quiet, haunted confession, Kaelen saw not a rival, but a soul carved by grief and bound by duty, fighting for more than herself. It twisted something deep inside him, recasting the Games not as contests of glory, but as brutal lifelines for worlds teetering on the edge.

Kaelen listened in stunned silence, the gravity of Lyra's confession pressing the air from his lungs. When he finally spoke, his voice was low, almost hoarse.

"I had no idea," he said. "We've all been playing at strategy and survival, but you... you've been carrying a war on your shoulders this entire time."

He met her eyes, not as a rival anymore, but as someone who recognized the raw shape of survival.

"You didn't have a choice. None of us did."

Lyra didn't answer, but her silence had changed. It wasn't cold now; it was dense with understanding, a shared burden neither of them could name. Kaelen felt the faintest give in her posture, like a blade easing a fraction back into its sheath.

Kaelen drew a careful breath, then continued. "I found something. In the stolen files, there are references to an organization working in the dark. I didn't know what it meant. Not until now."

Her head snapped toward him, eyes narrowing like blades. "You've seen proof?"

He nodded. "Enough to know they're real. And they're not just behind the Ascendance. They're dismantling everything, planet by planet."

Lyra looked away, her jaw clenched so tight it trembled. "Then, Mars was only the beginning."

An immense feeling of dread settled over Kaelen as the scope of it all crystallized. The conspiracy wasn't about rigging games for prestige. It was a methodical campaign of extinction; Mars had been their test. And now, the rest of the system waited in quiet ignorance for its turn.

The next few days blurred into a frantic race against time. Kaelen, Khel, and Lyra forged an uneasy alliance, brittle with old doubts, but held together by the stark weight of necessity. Suspicion still simmered beneath the surface, yet their shared urgency overpowered it, binding them tighter with each new revelation.

Jax was conspicuously absent from these councils. His brilliance was unquestioned, but the memory of his subtle manipulations lingered like a wound that hadn't healed cleanly.

Kaelen couldn't afford another fracture so close to the edge, not when every decision balanced the fate of worlds. Trust was too precious to gamble twice.

Theron, when present, contributed with clinical precision and nothing more; no allegiance, no confession. Kaelen watched him with a caution reserved for deep water; valuable, but unpredictable.

Together, they sifted through fragments of stolen data, intercepted transmissions, and cryptic records that only deepened the scope of their fears. Patterns emerged: encrypted coordinates, blacklisted cargo routes, covert directives all tied to a looming assault on Jupiter. The plan was staggering in its audacity: to destabilize the gas giant's fusion systems, setting off a catastrophic chain reaction that would obliterate Jovian infrastructure and send shock waves through the entire Solar System.

Kaelen stared at the simulation until his eyes watered: radiation belts flaring like open wounds; orbital stations torn from their tracks; atmospheric harvesters ripped apart by magnetospheric storms; debris avalanches chewing through habitations on the moons; millions displaced into dark, airless cold. Jupiter wasn't the prize. It was the first domino.

Their quiet rebellion drew support from unexpected places. Disillusioned members of the Ascendance Committee, once complicit by silence, recoiled at the monstrous scale of the conspiracy. Risking careers and lives, they threw their weight behind Kaelen's cause. They unlocked access to restricted archives, decrypted hidden channels, and exposed critical flaws in the Gauntlet's labyrinthine security. Some even arranged clandestine transport routes through corridors thick with surveillance.

They came to Kaelen one by one, faces drawn, voices tight. An archivist with shaking hands passing him a ring of clearance keys; a medic whispering two names and a docking time; a logistics officer deleting her own access history in front of him and saying, "If I vanish, don't go looking for me." Each act of courage bound the resistance closer and salted their resolve with a silent grief.

What began as a tenuous partnership bound by desperation evolved into something sharper, more deliberate. Their fragile coalition had been hardened into a true resistance.

As final plans took shape, Kaelen understood with startling clarity: this last confrontation wouldn't be a desperate gamble. It would be a calculated strike aimed straight at the heart of the conspiracy.

They prepared the contingencies that would outlive them if needed: encrypted data bursts queued on dead-man relays, evidence packets chained to timed uplinks across neutral networks. A final fail-safe, set to broadcast if they were unsuccessful.

In a dim maintenance bay that smelled faintly of stale smoke and oil, Kaelen, Khel, and Lyra shared a brief, wordless accord. It was not an oath, or grand vow, only the mutual recognition of what they were about to risk, and why.

Khel clasped Kaelen's forearm once, his grip tight and warm. Lyra checked her blade's edge and, for the first time, looked at Kaelen not as a burden or variable, but as a partner. It wasn't trust yet. But it was close enough.

Later, alone, Kaelen stood by the sealed viewplate and let the simulated starlight wash over his hands. He touched the small pouch of Earth soil at his belt, grounding himself in the one constant he still trusted. Helios had grown unnaturally quiet, its endless hum narrowed to a thin, waiting thread. Somewhere in the station's bones, the chronometer rolled over to the last cycle.

Kaelen pictured Jupiter's storms and the miners' lights threaded through the dark, the fragile chain of human brightness that made the void bearable. He thought of Mars bleeding under a false sun. He let the weight of it settle until it became something steadier: purpose.

They did not sleep. They sharpened their calm.

Nights were spent rehearsing routes that would more than likely collapse. They memorized names they might never say again, leaving their voices clear, and moved their fear into their fingers to be wielded like a weapon.

When the summons came, it would be subtle. Most likely an ordinary chime, a line of text, or perhaps a door unlocking. Until then, the station held its breath, and so did he. The Games began as a spectacle. But they would end in a reckoning.

Somewhere in the quiet, a soft tone bled through the air, unremarkable, almost tender. A door along the far corridor slid open with a polite sigh.

Kaelen lifted his eyes... the wait was over.

# FRACTURED MACHINE

I n the hours leading up to the trial, Helios felt unnaturally still. The corridors, usually alive with the hum of energy and conversation, lay hushed beneath a blanket of suspended tension. Even the air recyclers seemed to whisper more quietly, as though the station itself were holding its breath.

The competitors gathered in the wide antechamber outside the Labyrinth's sealed gates, each locked in their own rituals of tightening gear straps, re-calibrating visors, or pacing the floor in loops that betrayed their nerves. Kaelen stood close to Khel and Lyra, their fragile unity a thin bulwark against the gnawing edge of uncertainty. Around them, rival factions clustered in wary knots, eyes sharp, movements clipped. Even without words, the air vibrated with the promise of betrayal and final reckonings.

This was it—the culmination of every maneuver, every whispered alliance and quiet deceit that had come before. The silence before the end.

When the call finally came, it was almost anticlimactic: a hiss of pressurized locks, the soft mechanical sigh of reinforced doors parting. There was no speech, no grand announcement. Only the muted intake of breath as the competitors stepped forward, each knowing that none would emerge unchanged.

The air shimmered with heat as they crossed the threshold into the

Labyrinth, a living structure of light and machinery, equal parts marvel and menace. Its corridors pulsed faintly, veins of energy running beneath translucent surfaces that seemed to shift of their own accord. It wasn't a maze of stone or steel, but a sprawling organism of logic and pressure, designed to test not endurance, but unity.

The entrance loomed like a gate to another world: a towering arch of black obsidian, its surface etched with flowing sigils that glowed faintly in rhythm with the competitors' heartbeats.

Beyond it stretched darkness and the sound of a steady, mechanical heartbeat. Something vast and unseen.

The first chamber hit them like a storm. A vaulted expanse of interlaced conduits, flickering holographic panels, and rhythmic bursts of static discharge. The air reeked of stale ozone; the floor trembled like the pulse of a dying machine. At its center, a circular console blazed with cascading error codes. Flashing red and gold lights scrolled like frantic warning calls from a wounded mind.

The task at hand was glaringly clear: locate the fault, stabilize the flow and restore function before the countdown reached zero. Failure would mean a full system purge. No re-spawns, no simulations... just oblivion.

Hidden beneath the crackle of failing circuitry lay a deeper trial. This wasn't simply an engineering mistake. It was manipulation, a deliberate psychological crucible, designed to fracture what little trust remained. The conspirators, though weakened, had left their mark here. Suspicion, not machinery, was the true weapon.

Every debate over which conduit to seal first, every hesitation at the console, every glance exchanged under flickering light became another blade twisting into the fragile fabric of their alliance. Unity, their greatest strength, had been weaponized against them.

Jax moved first. He approached the console like a surgeon, his hands steady, every movement precise. His voice remained calm, analytical with no emotion as he plied. Each motion was so deliberate, it almost looked rehearsed.

Kaelen held back, eyes narrowed. He had seen where blind trust could lead, and Jax's calm efficiency still haunted him like an echo from the last betrayal. Instead of rushing to assist, Kaelen followed the conduits along the floor, tracing patterns in the tangled network of lights and pipes, seeking the system's rhythm rather than its noise.

Lyra bristled nearby, out of her element. Her power was built for decisive action, not the meticulous patience of diagnostics. Every blinking light seemed to taunt her.

"We're wasting time," she hissed, knuckles whitening around the railing.

Khel crouched beside a row of pressure valves, his massive frame moving with surprising delicacy. He tested seals and rerouted flow with the quiet intuition of someone who'd lived his life tending fragile systems deep in Jupiter's pressure mines. His voice rumbled low:

"Steady hands. We rush, we die."

Theron hovered near one of the holo-displays, parsing the chaos into order, his eyes flicking through data like a machine running probability threads. He spoke very little, mostly gestured, using a finger to trace patterns and every so often gave a soft click of his tongue. To him, this was just another problem to be solved.

Every second mattered. And every choice deepened the cracks between them.

Kaelen found himself challenging Jax's calls instinctively, proposing slower, safer alternatives that undermined the Satori's quick precision. He told himself it was prudence, but the truth was simpler; he didn't trust him. And the lack of trust bled into the air like a gas under pressure.

Lyra, unable to bear the debate, jumped into action. She forced open a sealed valve using only her bare hands. The metal screamed. Alarms blared. A blinding flare of energy cut through the chamber as the pressure spiked. The countdown began to accelerate.

"Damn it..." Kaelen huffed, lunging for the console.

"Stabilize the output!" Jax barked. "You've flooded the secondary core!"

"Then divert it!" Lyra snapped back. "You're the genius, aren't you?"

Theron's voice sliced through the chaos, flat and unshaken. "Focus. We lost sixty seconds arguing over nothing."

It worked... barely. Guided by Khel's steady control and Kaelen's quick recalibration, they rerouted the excess pressure through redundant loops. Warning lights dimmed one by one. The air was still thick with tension, but the machinery began to hum with restored rhythm.

For a fleeting moment, they moved as one.

Despite the cracks, their skills aligned like folds of the same blade. Jax's technical mastery, Khel's intuition, Lyra's raw force, Theron's foresight, and Kaelen's quiet diplomacy all interlocked in an improbable balance.

Kaelen found himself mediating on instinct, defusing the sharp edges of anger, redirecting focus, keeping them from collapsing inward.

When the final sequence clicked into place and the chamber lights steadied, a low chime rolled through the Labyrinth. System restored. Timer halted.

They had done it...

But the victory felt hollow, like a breath stolen before the plunge.

Kaelen looked at each of them, reading exhaustion, suspicion, pride and relief. For a heartbeat, he saw what they could have been if not for the rot beneath all of it, a team strong enough to move worlds.

Lyra exhaled slowly, her gaze distant. "That was the first chamber," she murmured. "How many more?"

Theron's fingers hovered over the now quiet holo-display. "Enough," he said quietly, "to make us choose what matters most."

No one spoke after that. The air between them had changed. It became denser, heavier and charged with the awareness that survival would not be enough this time.

They pressed on, moving through the next corridor, the hum of machinery fading into something almost sentient; the soft, rhythmic pulse of a test that wasn't finished with them yet.

The light coming from the restored chamber dimmed behind them, swallowed up by the dark pulse ahead, a grim warning that each step forward would demand more than the last.

# TRIAL OF TRUST

They pressed deeper into the Labyrinth, each chamber more punishing than the last. One trial challenged their coordination in zero gravity, where spinning platforms and drifting debris demanded split-second timing and seamless teamwork. Another hurled them into a hyper-realistic simulation where the laws of physics bent unpredictably, forcing them to adapt to constantly shifting realities.

A third chamber transformed into a game of interstellar chess, each move reshaping a dynamic battlefield in real time, a ruthless test of foresight and restraint. But the most harrowing challenge came not from physical trials or tactical puzzles, but from moral dilemmas: holographic scenarios that pitted logic against empathy and duty against conscience.

Each test pushed them to the edge, not just physically or mentally, but emotionally. Trust became a scarce currency, and cooperation, a lifeline. Amid the strain of cerebral combat, something unexpected began to take root: a grudging respect, forged in adversity, slowly knitting fractured bonds back together through shared survival.

The Labyrinth was more than a series of challenges; it was a psychological siege. Its very architecture seemed designed to erode trust. Familiar voices whispered secrets from unseen corners. Shadows shifted with intent, moving in ways that defied logic. Every step deeper into the maze felt less like progress and more like descent, into doubt, into suspicion, into a test of loyalty itself.

Alliances wavered under the pressure of things left unsaid. The air grew dense with unease; each chamber laced with the threat of unseen consequences. And Kaelen couldn't shake the feeling that the Labyrinth was sentient, watching, adapting, turning their fears against them.

What once seemed like isolated manipulations now echoed as part of a greater design. Deception clung to every surface, not as a tactic used by one rival, but as the very fabric of the maze itself. The Labyrinth wasn't just a test of strength or intellect; it was a crucible of trust, and its purpose was far darker than any of them had imagined.

In one particularly harrowing chamber, the challenge turned lethal. What first appeared to be a harmless logic puzzle revealed itself as a trap: an intricate grid of laser beams, each capable of instant vaporization. The objective was to position a set of reflective crystals, redirecting the beams into a safe configuration. One misstep meant certain death.

Theron, calm and methodical, quickly devised a solution—sound, elegant, and mathematically precise. But Kaelen hesitated. The memory of past manipulations surfaced, clouding his judgment. Rather than trust the plan, he proposed an alternate route that was riskier, less refined, but free from Jax's influence.

Jax, eyes gleaming with quiet amusement, leaned into the tension. "Let him lead," he said, just loud enough to plant doubt. "Let's see what kind of strategist Earth really produces." It wasn't encouragement; it was provocation, a weaponized whisper designed to destabilize.

With pride and suspicion warring in his chest, Kaelen stepped forward into the deadly maze, unaware of just how close he was to confirming his worst fears.

The gamble had worked; barely. They escaped with the puzzle solved, but only by the thinnest margin. The corridor behind them pulsed with residual heat, a silent reminder of how close they'd come to failure.

The brush with death struck Kaelen deeply. He was forced to confront the cost of mistrust, to realize that his refusal to rely on others had nearly doomed them all. In that moment, paranoia gave way to clarity. Strategy alone wasn't enough. Leadership demanded something more: the courage to believe in others, even when belief felt like the greatest risk of all.

Jax offered no gloating remarks. Instead, he watched Kaelen with a calculating stillness, a flicker of something unreadable crossing his face. Was it approval perhaps, or quiet vindication? "Close call," he said finally, his tone cool but not unkind. "Next time, maybe we skip the part where we almost die proving a point."

Kaelen didn't respond. He didn't need to. The truth was already settled between them, sharp, uncomfortable, and undeniable.

The last chamber tested exactly that.

It offered no puzzles, no physics-defying traps, only choice. A sequence of moral dilemmas, each more harrowing than the last. Sacrifice personal safety or risk the group. Shield a comrade or expose a lie. Choose loyalty or choose the future of the Solar System. The test wasn't one of strength or intellect; it was of integrity, empathy, and the courage to rise above division. In the Labyrinth's crucible, these decisions became mirrors, reflecting not who they wanted to be, but who they truly were.

In the end, they emerged victorious. Together, they had overcome the Labyrinth's relentless trials with a fragile blend of skill, resolve, and uneasy cooperation. But the triumph rang hollow.

The maze had stripped away the last illusions. It had exposed the cracks in their alliances, the corrosive reach of ambition, and the tenuous strands of trust pulled taut under pressure. For Kaelen, the experience crystallized a bitter truth: the Ascendance was never just a competition of strength or cunning; it was a crucible of manipulation, where loyalty was bartered, and betrayal lurked behind every smile.

And beneath it all, the conspiracy endured, silent, coiled, waiting. Its influence threaded through the competition like an invisible snare, tightening with each victory. Kaelen had survived this test, but the outcome felt more like a warning than a reward.

The alliance—tempered by adversity but still fragile—might not withstand what came next. The final battle was no longer about triumph; it was about truth. And in the storm to come, trust would either be their greatest weapon... or their fatal flaw.

Kaelen's hand brushed the small pouch of Earth soil at his belt, the faint grit catching against his skin, a quiet reminder that even in the labyrinth's shifting dark, something real endured.

# CRUCIBLE: ISOLATION

**H**elios bled away around them, the last echo of the Labyrinth's sterile lights swallowed by a horizon of ash. The floor shuddered, the walls unraveled into a seam of glare, and then the world snapped cold.

The shimmering walls of the Labyrinth dissolved, replaced by a bleak, unforgiving landscape. Gone were the shifting illusions and engineered corridors; now stretched a barren plain under a twilight sky, jagged rocks tearing through cracked soil like the bones of a dead world. The air stung with the smell of ozone and dust, a sharp reminder of the desolation beneath the Ascendance's polished veneer.

This was The Crucible. A trial meant to break them before the end came.

Unlike those before it, this was not designed to test intellect or skill. It was built to shatter resolve, sever alliances, and expose what remained when hope ran dry. The rules were brutal in their simplicity: survive. Resources were scarce. The terrain, merciless. Storms struck without warning, and environmental hazards waited behind every jagged ridge. But the greatest threat wasn't the land; it was the others.

The trial began with a cruel illusion of order: a solitary survival phase designed to isolate each competitor and test their resilience. Armed only with a basic survival kit, they had a limited window to secure food, water, and shelter. On the surface, it seemed straightforward.

But isolation wasn't just a condition; it was the first strike. A silent weapon meant to unearth buried grudges, rekindle betrayals, and amplify every doubt sown in the Labyrinth.

Kaelen battled not only the harsh terrain but the unease clawing at his thoughts. The sting of Theron's confession hadn't faded, and Jax's accusations still echoed like a low drumbeat in the back of his mind. Every step through the dust-blown wasteland felt heavy with suspicion. Even as he scavenged supplies, conserved rations, and patched together a crude shelter, his attention never strayed far from the threat that might come. Not from the storm, but from someone he once called an ally.

In the beginning, the rivalry had felt clean, almost noble. A contest of skill, of vision, of leadership. He remembered the early verbal clashes with Lyra, sharp and strategic, each probing for weakness beneath polished diplomacy. Theron had been the inscrutable foil, always two steps ahead, maddening in his precision.

Even Jax, chaotic and aloof, seemed more provocateur than threat. But the Crucible had stripped the theater away. Their rivalry no longer lived in words or tactics; it lived in suspicion, betrayal, and the growing fear that the real game had started long before the Ascendance ever did.

He pressed onward, the wind whipping across the desolate plain, turning grit to glass against his skin. Hours bled into one another beneath the dim twilight, his sense of time eroding with each hollow footstep. Fatigue gnawed at the edges of his focus. He hadn't eaten since morning; his water ration was dangerously low.

The whisper came faintly and suddenly, carried on the wind like a memory: "You were warned."

Kaelen spun, heart slamming against his ribs. No one was there. Nothing but cracked stone and dust behind him.

He told himself it was the wind... just the wind. But as he turned to continue, a flicker of movement danced in the corner of his eye: a silhouette, half-seen behind a jagged ridge. Tall. Still. Watching.

"Jax?" he called out instinctively. No answer.

He scrambled up the slope, but the ridge was empty. No footprints. No heat signature on his scanner. Just rocks and an eerie silence, broken only by the rushing wind.

Doubt twisted in his chest. Was it exhaustion? A trick of the light? Or something more calculated? Was someone playing with him, testing his nerves? The labyrinth had taught him to question what was real. This place, whatever it was, seemed determined to unmake him one thought at a time. He tightened his grip on his staff and kept moving, wary now not just of enemies in the field, but phantoms in his mind.

He blinked hard, trying to clear the mirage from his mind. The memory, if that's what it was faded like smoke, but the unease it stirred refused to leave. Maybe it had been a hallucination brought on by dehydration mixed with exhaustion. Or maybe something deeper was unraveling. Either way, he knew he couldn't afford to lose focus now. Not here. Not this close.

He forced the image from his mind and turned his attention outward. If he couldn't trust his own thoughts, he would have to trust what he could observe, what he could verify. And what he saw unsettled him.

Khel, as poised and unshakable as ever, adapted to the simulation with unsettling precision. He constructed a fully functional shelter within hours, expertly navigating the nuances of the Crucible's harsh terrain. His uncanny efficiency, once a source of admiration, now sparked renewed suspicion.

Was it simply skill honed through years of work beneath Jupiter's crushing systems, or something more calculated? Perhaps a performance meant to mask deeper, more sinister intentions? Kaelen watched him closely but found no simple answers.

Lyra, meanwhile, kept to the shadows, observant, methodical, and increasingly volatile. Her distrust of Theron had hardened into a quiet, burning animosity. She moved through the simulation like a predator, gathering supplies with practiced efficiency while avoiding contact. But she wasn't just surviving. She was building a case. Every interaction, every subtle maneuver, every suspicious glance was recorded in her mind like evidence in a trial. And the picture forming in her head was damning.

Theron remained an enigma, impervious to the growing tide of suspicion. He moved with calm precision; his every action deliberate. The accusations seemed to glance off him, unacknowledged and unanswered. His silence wasn't mere stoicism; it was armor, forged through necessity, a way of shielding himself from the poisonous atmosphere of mistrust. Whether it was arrogance or self-preservation, no one could say for certain.

The isolation phase didn't last. As resources dwindled and the environment grew increasingly lethal, the illusion of independence crumbled. The first major test came with a simulated sandstorm. A violent, swirling vortex of grit and fury that descended without warning, it tore through the landscape like a living beast, threatening to entomb them all.

Cooperation became unavoidable. Temporary alliances were forged from necessity; delicate truces held together by desperation and the primal instinct to survive. These fragile collaborations were riddled with tension. Every helpful act carried the weight of suspicion. Each shared ration and every word offered in support was measured against the possibility of betrayal. Kindness no longer felt like a virtue; it had become a tactic, one that might mask a deeper scheme.

The air between them crackled with distrust. Every gesture could be a feint. Every alliance was a coin toss between trust and treachery.

They lashed shelters to fractured rock, braced fabric tense against screaming gusts, and shared the scant warmth of body heat as static snapped blue along the edges of their makeshift camps. The storm's roar swallowed conversation, reduced intention to touch and motion. In the fury of a complete whiteout, they learned again how thin a line survival could be.

By the time the wind relented, their faces were raw, their throats scraped by dust. The Crucible had taken its first pound of flesh and offered nothing in return.

Khel's voice rasped beside him, barely audible over the fading wind. "Still breathing?"

Kaelen nodded, the motion stiff and subtle. "For now."

Khel gave a thin smile, lines of grit tracing the corner of his mouth. "Then we're winning."

The storm's fury had passed, but the silence it left behind was worse. It wasn't peace; it was pressure, waiting for the next fracture.

# CRUCIBLE: RECKONING

I n the uneasy calm after the storm, the Crucible bared a more subtle set of teeth.

Selene knelt by a collapsed relay drone, its casing pitted and scored by static discharge. She pried it open with surgical precision; her hands remained steady, but her eyes were distant. Kaelen approached, expecting her usual guarded composure, and caught something else instead: a flicker of vulnerability, quickly shuttered.

"This whole trial," she murmured, not looking up, "isn't about survival. It's about pressure and evaluating who fractures and who pretends not to." She paused, then added, almost too quiet to hear, "I've worn the mask so long, I'm not sure I'd recognize the fracture if it came." A beat later, she closed the panel and stood up, her face once again unreadable. "Let's not give them the satisfaction."

When the second phase began, it struck at their moral core.

A simulated distress signal echoed from a cave near the edge of the encampment. Words were fragmented, static-laced, riddled with desperation. Its source was untraceable. Its legitimacy, unverifiable. Was it a genuine cry for help, or a trap laid by the simulation... or worse, by one of their own?

The choice was a test of conscience: intervene and risk annihilation or walk away and live with the weight of leaving someone to their demise.

It wasn't a cut and dry discussion in the least. The debate that followed was intense and emotionally charged.

Lyra, ever the cynic, argued forcefully against responding. "We walk in there," she growled, "we don't walk out." To her, trust was a liability, and the signal reeked of deception.

Theron, his usual pragmatism tempered by a rare flicker of compassion, pushed back. "If we turn our backs now," he said quietly, "what are we even fighting for?"

Khel, true to form, offered no opinion. He stood apart, eyes scanning each speaker with unnerving detachment, calculating odds behind every word.

Kaelen stood at the center of the storm, torn between caution and conviction. His diplomatic instincts urged him to act, to lead with courage, to show that compassion still had a place in survival. But reason whispered restraint. One wrong move or misplaced trust could doom them all.

This decision, made under the crushing weight of doubt and risk, would become a defining moment, not just in the competition, but in Kaelen's evolution as a leader.

The storm howled again along the ridge-lines, a violent mirror of their internal chaos. Every step forward in the Crucible was taken under the gaze of rivals and of unseen puppeteers pulling invisible strings from the shadows. Right and wrong no longer existed in the absolute. This was no longer just a competition. It was a battle for their souls, and a fight for the future.

They had made their choice.

No one announced it. No vote was called. The silence stretched, then folded in on itself as they turned from the mouth of the cave and resumed repairs, rationing, the endless arithmetic of survival. If there had been a life within that darkness, it would be beyond their reach now. If there had been a trap, it would have been denied its prize.

As they turned away, a faint sound followed them out of the cave, one long exhale that might have been wind, or might have been something else entirely. No one spoke of it. They didn't need to. The silence said enough.

In the uneasy calm that followed, Kaelen grappled with more than exhaustion. The challenges hadn't just stripped them bare; they had exposed fractures that ran deeper than any single trial. They never spoke of the cave again. Not openly. But something unspoken settled over them in the silence that followed. There was a tension that hadn't been there before.

Kaelen caught it in Lyra's narrowed eyes, in the way Theron avoided his gaze for once, his calm no longer an anchor but a shield. Even Khel, normally inscrutable, kept glancing toward the horizon as if expecting something, or someone, that never came.

Whether the signal had been real was no longer of any consequence. What mattered was the choice they had made together... or failed to. And whatever had waited in that darkness, be it trap or truth, it was gone now. Their moment had passed. The Crucible had moved on, but its weight remained.

They stood on fragile ground, haunted by decisions made in desperation, with their loyalty tested to the breaking point. Every glance between them carried an unspoken question. Every silence felt heavier. And somewhere beyond their immediate struggles, Kaelen could feel the pulse of something vast and hidden, tightening its grip around him, an orchestration larger than any single trial.

The Crucible had done what it was built for: to pare them down to what was left when certainty died. In the gathering dusk, as ash skittered across the hardpan and the wind stitched thin lines over the sand, Kaelen understood that the next move would not be granted by the arena. It would be taken.

And as he felt the last of his certainty crumble, he realized Selene had been right from the start; pressure didn't just fracture; it revealed what was already broken.

Whether they deserved it, or survived it, would be decided by what they trusted when nothing else held.

# CLUES FROM THE PAST

The Labyrinth had been a victory, but it left a bitter taste. Close calls, veiled agendas, and crumbling trust suggested something deeper, something far more insidious than competition alone. The alliance, forged under the weight of necessity, now felt brittle, strained by fractures that no longer seemed incidental.

Theron's manipulations, Jax's calculated provocations, and Lyra's guarded volatility didn't feel like personal quirks anymore. They felt like calculated moves in a larger game, orchestrated by forces still hidden in the shadows.

And the conspiracy, once a distant whisper behind the roar of the Games, was now a constant presence, humming at the edges of every silence, growing louder with each passing trial. Kaelen could no longer ignore it. The patterns were there, coiling like threads through every challenge, every betrayal.

Even victory had become suspect. If the Games were designed to forge champions, why did they feel more like survivors crawling from the wreckage?

Their next destination offered a rare reprieve from the physical trials: the Archives of Old Tyme. Suspended in the asteroid belt between Mars and Jupiter, it was a relic of a bygone age, a sprawling library station where centuries of interstellar history slept beneath layers of dust and encrypted code. Here were the chronicles of Ascendance past: official records, forgotten comms, encrypted journals, even mythic fragments dismissed as propaganda or allegory.

To most, the Archives were a ceremonial detour. To Kaelen, they were a chance. If the truth had roots, they would be buried here. And if the conspiracy had a beginning, this was where the trail might finally emerge from the shadows.

The transport docked in near silence, its engines winding down like an exhale after too long a breath. The Archives of Old Tyme loomed, an enormous, drifting structure of tarnished alloy and crystalline domes, orbiting a lonely asteroid like a relic forgotten by time. As Kaelen stepped off the platform, the air grew still, as if the very station were holding its breath.

Inside, the halls were dim and echoing, filled with shelves and holotables, the walls lined with flickering data reels and ancient symbols from a dozen cultures. Every corridor carried the faint hum of machines older than any of them, their upkeep patchwork at best.

Dust floated in the artificial light, stirred by footsteps that felt too loud in the oppressive silence. It wasn't just a place of knowledge; it felt like a tomb, as if every secret housed here had died long before they arrived. Kaelen's hand brushed against the small pouch of soil tucked discreetly inside his uniform, his mother's gift, the reminder of Earth's endurance. In this mausoleum of lost truths, he needed that anchor more than ever.

Kaelen began with the official records, sifting meticulously through decades of Ascendance transcripts. The reports were sterile lists of winners, descriptions of challenges, final scores, all written in the clinical language of bureaucratic neutrality.

But a strange pattern emerged: a disproportionate number of past competitors had vanished or died under suspicious circumstances not long after their triumphs. Official causes ranged from transport malfunctions to sudden illness and even "self-inflicted harm," but the frequency and the vagueness were too unsettling to dismiss. These weren't isolated tragedies. They were echoes of something darker.

Unsatisfied, Kaelen turned his attention to the unpolished undercurrent of the Archives: the personal journals, fringe news bulletins, and oral histories preserved by descendants of former competitors. These unofficial sources were rampant with speculation but rich in details the more formal records conveniently left out.

Here, he unearthed whispers of secret factions, hidden allegiances, and a long-standing power struggle that reached far beyond the Games. Repeatedly, one name surfaced: the Obsidian Order, a shadowy organization said to have infiltrated and manipulated the Ascendance for generations. Its ties pointed unmistakably toward Pluto. Finally, they uncovered the true name of the conspirators' organization.

Theron initially scoffed at the rumors, dismissing them as speculative fantasy, stories spun by bitter competitors and conspiracy theorists alike. But Kaelen's relentless digging, paired with several disturbing discoveries, chipped away at his skepticism.

In a weathered journal penned by a Jovian finalist from the 22nd-century Ascendance, Kaelen found a cryptic entry describing a hidden chamber buried deep within the Labyrinth. The room, absent from any official blueprints, was said to house a relic, an ancient artifact rumored to unlock forgotten technologies capable of reshaping the very balance of power across the Solar System.

Ever attuned to opportunity, Theron latched onto the revelation with renewed interest. He proposed that the Obsidian Order had been using the artifact to manipulate the outcomes of the Ascendance for generations. Elevating chosen winners, silencing dissenters, and steering the course of history from the shadows.

His own studies into obscure Neydrin myths supported the theory: stories of forbidden knowledge and celestial alignments that opened a hidden portal at the edge of the system. All signs, legend and record alike, seemed to converge on Pluto, the cold and distant world cloaked in mystery.

Meanwhile, Lyra turned her focus to more tangible threats. Drawing from classified Martian dossiers and black-market archives, she uncovered chilling evidence of assassinations, disappearances, and sabotage linked to earlier competitions.

The pattern was too precise to be random. Advanced weaponry and off-ledger military tech had been deployed, not just to gain an edge in the Games, but to eliminate competitors who had seen too much or come too close to the truth. These weren't isolated incidents. They were surgical strikes, executed with purpose and precision.

Jax listened in stony silence, arms folded, his gaze fixed on the glowing holomap of the outer planets. When Pluto was mentioned, something in his expression shifted, barely noticeable, but not lost on Kaelen.

"If the Orders reach extends that far," he said finally, his voice low and clinical, "then it's not just political influence we're dealing with. It's systemic control of technological advancement. Entire generations of progress... diverted, hoarded."

There was a glint in his eye, not fear, but something closer to fascination. The prospect of lost science, hidden schematics and suppressed breakthroughs. This was a puzzle worthy of his intellect. And perhaps, Kaelen realized, a temptation as dangerous as the conspiracy itself.

Kaelen's gaze lingered on him, wary. He couldn't deny Jax's brilliance or the precision of his insights. But he also couldn't forget how close Jax had come to fracturing them in the Labyrinth. Trust remained out of reach. For now, he would use Jax's mind as a tool, but nothing more.

As their investigation deepened, fragments of information scattered across journals, forgotten data caches, and obscure myths aligned. A chilling picture emerged. The Plutonian conspiracy, as they called it, reached far beyond a single competition. It was about control over access to ancient, forbidden technologies capable of reshaping the balance of power across the Solar System.

The Obsidian Order had been operating from the shadows for centuries, using the Ascendance as both a proving ground and a cover used for recruiting the useful, discarding the rest, and quietly steering the course of interstellar politics to serve their own ends.

Theron stood stiff and motionless as the implications settled around them, his usual calm posture now tense with unease. His silence was no longer armor; it was calculation. He had always maneuvered in the shadows, but this level of subterfuge unnerved even him. The strategist in him recognized the brilliance of the design. The man beneath it quietly feared what he was now up against.

Jax leaned in, eyes gleaming, captivated more than alarmed. He traced the cipher's structure with his fingers, reverent in the way only an engineer obsessed with systems could be. As the cipher resolved into meaning, the ambient hum of the Archives seemed to falter, as if even the ancient machinery understood the gravity of what they'd uncovered. Dust drifted in the still air, suspended like the breath of the dead.

"It's elegant," he murmured, almost admiringly. "Brutally so." His mind had already leapt beyond the conspiracy, wondering how the artifact worked, what technologies it touched, and whether he could outsmart it. But even his curiosity couldn't mask the weight in his voice. For once, brilliance offered no comfort.

Lyra's expression darkened with every connection made. The soldier in her saw no mystery, but motive. This wasn't politics; it was war. "Of course," she muttered, more to herself than to anyone else. "That's why they silenced the Martian council. That's why they turned the Games into a culling ground." Her distrust, already bone-deep, became something colder. She wasn't just suspicious now; she was preparing for a reckoning.

Khel said nothing, but his stillness spoke volumes. He stared at the decoded names, the false victories, the fabricated losses, his jaw set in quiet disapproval. He had lived his life among buried secrets and dangerous truths. This he understood almost instinctively. And yet, even for him, the scale of it was sobering. He met Kaelen's gaze once, and the look they exchanged needed no words. There would be no going back.

It wasn't long before there came a breakthrough that changed everything. The historical documents, once dismissed as sterile accounts of winners and trials, held more than just records. Beneath their procedural language lay a concealed system of encryption, sophisticated, layered, and deliberately buried. Woven through the names of winners, challenge structures, and scoring anomalies was a hidden cipher. It wasn't meant to reveal the truth. It had been designed to bury it.

Once decrypted, the implications struck like a thunderclap. Every message spoke of a vast interconnected network. Not just a single organization, but a web of operatives embedded across multiple planetary governments, all united under the banner of the Obsidian Order. Their reach was extended farther than anyone could have imagined. They had infiltrated the highest seats of power, rewritten the rules of the Ascendance, and turned a system meant to celebrate merit into a tool of silent domination.

The hidden chamber in the Labyrinth. The ancient artifact. The string of vanished competitors. Each thread, once isolated, now wove into a tapestry of long-game manipulation and ruthless control. What they had uncovered wasn't just a conspiracy; it was the scaffolding of a centuries-old shadow regime shaping the future of the Solar System.

The revelation was both exhilarating and terrifying. The Ascendance, once thought a crucible of unity and ambition, had become a stage for a hidden war. And now, Kaelen and his fragile alliance stood squarely in the center of it; outnumbered, outmaneuvered, but no longer blind.

They weren't fighting for personal glory anymore; they were fighting to expose the truth, to protect their worlds from a shadow war decades in the making. The fragile trust forged in the fires of the Labyrinth would now face its ultimate trial. The organization was no longer a whisper in the dark. It had a name. The Obsidian Order was watching, waiting, and ready to strike.

Kaelen stood at the edge of the archive chamber, the weight of history pressing down around him. The path forward was uncertain, the dangers immense, but for the first time, the fight had clarity. He touched the small pouch at his belt, the soil of a forgotten Earth warm against his palm, a reminder that truth, once buried, could still take root.

No more guessing. No more shadows. Now, they had something to aim at.

And Kaelen would not let them vanish quietly into the void.

# DESIGNS OF RUIN

The decoded messages, painstakingly extracted from centuries of mundane competition records, painted a chilling portrait. The Obsidian Order was no monolithic empire, but a decentralized network, with tendrils embedded deep within the political and economic structures of every major planet.

Their influence operated in the shadows, through subtle manipulation, rather than conquest: strategic disinformation, quietly forged alliances, and the careful placement of loyal operatives in key positions of authority.

They were beyond seeking power for power's sake. Their vision was much darker. They wanted total collapse, the slow erosion of unity and the complete disintegration of the Solar Concordance. From that fracture, they would unleash nothing but chaos.

Their ideology, pieced together from intercepted communications and fragmented texts, was a disturbing fusion of anarchism and radical utopianism. They believed the Solar Concordance, a system built on cooperation and mutual resource-sharing, was a fragile illusion. In their eyes, the natural order of intelligent life was not peace, but competition. Suppressing that drive only delayed the inevitable: a catastrophic war born of resentment.

The Order's solution was grotesque in its logic. They would speed up the breakdown, catalyze the conflict, and allow the system to burn down. From its ashes, they would build a new order: raw and ruthless, governed by strength and cunning.

It wasn't peace they wanted. It was evolution through destruction.

For Kaelen, that revelation carried a terrible symmetry. The Games themselves, every test, every betrayal, every moral fracture, had reflected that same creed. The Ascendance wasn't entertainment or diplomacy dressed in spectacle. It had been the incubator of the Obsidian philosophy all along: a living experiment proving that chaos produced the most adaptable survivors.

The methods the Order used were just as terrifying as its ideology. The Ascendance, once thought to be a trial of merit and endurance, was in truth a curated arena, used as a recruitment ground for the Obsidian Order. Here, they scouted individuals of exceptional potential, watching closely to determine who could be manipulated... and who posed too great a threat. The disappearances, the assassinations, the "accidents" that marred the competition's history were not isolated tragedies, but precision strikes, calculated eliminations designed to clear the path for their grand design.

Their aim emerged from a chilling passage buried in the forgotten archives of an ancient Plutonian species known as the Uthraxi. It spoke of an incomprehensible, devastating weapon capable of disrupting the gravitational equilibrium of the solar system itself. This weapon, seemingly tied to the artifact hidden deep within the Labyrinth's secret chamber, held the power to bend space and time, to tear reality at its seams.

The Obsidian Order believed that with it, they could plunge the system into chaos by collapsing empires, toppling planetary alliances, and resetting civilization. From the wreckage, only the ruthless would rise. From that ruin, they intended to build their "new dawn."

The discovery struck their fragile alliance like a seismic shockwave. Khel, ever the paragon of composure, allowed a rare flicker of fear to surface. Jax, opportunist though he was, seemed genuinely shaken by the sheer magnitude of the conspiracy they had uncovered. Theron stood, hardened and unshakable in grim silence, letting the reality of their situation sink in. But Kaelen felt something else arise within him: a steady, unrelenting determination.

He hadn't asked for this war, but the moment he glimpsed its scale, he knew retreat would never be an option. The burden had shifted. It was no longer just about survival or the competition. It was about his duty to Earth, to the allies he trusted, and to the fragile balance of peace across the Solar System.

For a long, tense moment, the Archives seemed to hold their collective breath. Dust hung motionless in the low light. Even the old data-cores hummed more softly, as if the station itself was listening. The silence that followed was heavy, not with fear, but with purpose sharpening into inevitability.

Kaelen stood apart from the others, staring at the flickering holomap of the outer worlds. The threads of conspiracy had finally taken shape, and in that fragile moment of clarity, he felt the shift within himself, the quiet acceptance that they were no longer contestants in a game, but soldiers in a hidden war. Whatever came next would not be staged for the audience. It would be real.

The next trial arrived without warning, announced in the clipped neutrality of the Overseer's voice.

Deep within the station, a power relay groaned to life, echoing through the steel like a pulse. One by one, the lights dimmed, as if the Archives themselves were bracing for what was coming. The air felt charged and stretched thin, their anticipation turning slowly into dread.

They were herded into a circular chamber whose walls rippled with mirrored glass. The challenge was introduced as a test of "diplomatic perception", a simulation designed to assess how well they could distinguish truth from fabrication in the shifting landscape of interplanetary politics.

At first, the exercise seemed straightforward. Competitors were handed dossiers, each filled with treaties, resource contracts, and encrypted communications between rival factions. Their task was to determine which were genuine and which had been falsified.

But the deeper Kaelen delved, the more insidious the test revealed itself to be.

The dossiers weren't about abstract governments or distant planets; they were about them.

Each packet contained accusations implicating members of their own fragile alliance: falsified betrayals, fabricated secret deals, messages written to appear as if their allies had been whispering to the Obsidian Order all along.

Theron was presented as having orchestrated a hidden contract with Neydrin warlords. Lyra's file suggested back-channel arms trades with Martian separatists. Jax's folder dripped with engineered records of technological theft, implicating him in sabotages that had never occurred. Even Kaelen wasn't spared. The documents alleged clandestine communications with Earth's military hierarchy, suggesting his role in the Ascendance was little more than a political smokescreen.

The air thickened with suspicion. Eyes narrowed. Hands hovered too long near weapons. It was a trap not designed to test knowledge, but to fracture them from within.

Khel's jaw tightened as he scanned the fabricated reports implicating him in Jovian corruption. He didn't speak at first, but the set of his shoulders betrayed the storm behind his stoic mask. Lyra slammed her file down with a growl, pacing like a caged predator. Jax laughed at his accusations, but the sound was brittle, forced, his eyes flicking warily to Theron.

Kaelen felt the air bending, trust unraveling thread by thread. The Order wasn't testing their ability to detect lies, it was testing how easily they could be broken by them.

Drawing on every ounce of composure, Kaelen raised his voice above the growing tension.

"This is theater," he said, steady but firm. "They want us to believe the worst of each other because it's the quickest way to end us without lifting a blade. If we let these pages dictate our choices, then we've already lost."

His words didn't erase the suspicion, but they gave the others pause enough for him to press on.

"We verify everything. Together. Every claim, every record. We dismantle the lies as a team, not alone."

It took agonizing hours of cross-checking, arguing, and challenging one another before the falsehoods became apparent. Patterns repeated too neatly. Timelines clashed subtly but fatally. Encrypted strings recycled where randomness should have reigned. Piece by piece, they tore through the illusions.

When the last deception collapsed, the mirrored walls dissolved into empty black, and the Overseer's voice returned.

"Trial complete. Survivors: all."

It sounded like victory. But Kaelen knew better.

The simulation hadn't truly tested their perception; it had tested their faith. And though they had survived, something in the way Lyra avoided Theron's gaze, or how Jax smirked a little too long at Kaelen's file, told him the damage had been done.

In the heavy quiet that followed, Kaelen reached unconsciously for the small pouch of soil at his belt. The grains pressed against his palm, cool and grounding. He closed his eyes, anchoring himself to its weight... to something real. Around him, the chamber was silent, but the echo of the Order's design lingered like smoke.

Trust was still alive, but just barely.

And the Games, Kaelen realized, were no longer a contest of strength or survival. They had become the battlefield of truth itself.

# SEEDS OF RESISTANCE

Tension cracked across the room like static.

Aris, her eyes sharp with suspicion, jabbed a finger toward the simulation holomap. "And how do we know we're not playing right into their hands? Planting messages, digging through archives, chasing whispers... they wanted us to find this. This isn't a trial; it's a damn trap. If even one faction thinks we're manipulating perceptions, the whole alliance will fracture."

Jax folded his arms, keeping his mouth tight. "It has to look organic. That's the only way we slip truth past the Order's censors. You want to pull punches now, Aris? After everything?"

"Enough," Lyra cut in, voice taut. "We can't afford any fractures."

But the words did little to calm the current gnawing at them.

Before another argument could flare, Selene moved between them with quiet grace; a stillness that silenced the room more effectively than shouting ever could. Placing one hand gently on the edge of the table, she spoke with a voice barely above a whisper, yet commanding in its clarity.

"Truth," she said softly, "doesn't need to be loud to be heard."

All eyes turned to her.

"We've all lost something," she continued. "Homes. Friends. Ideals we thought to be unshakable. And now we stand on the edge of another loss... trust."

Her gaze moved from Aris to Jax without judgment. "Fear divides. That's what the Order counts on. But clarity, even when we disagree, is strength. We don't have to agree on every tactic, but we do need to believe in the goal."

Kaelen watched her, the pressure in his chest easing again. Selene didn't raise her voice or make demands. She simply shifted the emotional gravity of the room. Her words weren't a plea. They were an anchor.

Selene drew in a quiet breath. "Yes, we let the Games be our arena. But we have to let our unity be the real performance. Subtle, unshakable, and most of all, visible."

Aris gave a tight nod, the fire in her expression cooling to resolve. "Then we do it right. No shortcuts. No collateral."

Jax muttered something under his breath. "Fine. Precision only. No theater."

Selene stepped back, reserved and without gesture. Her point had been made, and more importantly, accepted.

The silence surrounding the group carried an unfamiliar weight. Outside, the soft hum of Helios' systems pressed against the walls, a reminder that the Games went on, indifferent to what they plotted within its chambers. For the first time, their unity no longer felt reactive. It had become deliberate; defiance forged into strategy.

Their next step had to be precise. A direct accusation against the Obsidian Order would be reckless. Many of its agents hid in plain sight, their influence woven deep into the institutions meant to protect the system.

The evidence they possessed, while damning, was scattered and circumstantial at best, easily dismissed or buried. They needed a different approach. A comprehensive plan to expose the conspiracy from within, to set a trap so undeniable, so public, that not even the Orders reach could smother it. It would be dangerous... perhaps fatal.

But at this point, it was the only way forward.

Theron, drawing from his thorough grasp of Neydrin subterfuge, proposed a bold and treacherous plan. They would weaponize the very arena the Obsidian Order had used for centuries—Helios itself.

Each remaining stage would become a platform, a carefully crafted theater where slivers of truth could be slipped into the light, veiled in spectacle. They would plant clues as provocations, nudging the audience, the officials, and the competitors toward revelations they could not ignore. It was a high-wire act of timing, misdirection, and psychological warfare aimed at turning the Order's own rules against them.

Their first opportunity came with the Diplomatic Negotiations challenge, a simulated interstellar summit meant to test the competitors' political finesse. Here, Theron saw the perfect opening. They would embed fragments of evidence, intercepted communications, falsified treaties and covert directives directly into the simulation. Every single piece of evidence would point subtly to known affiliates of the Obsidian Order: officials from powerful planetary governments with dark allegiances.

Hidden within innocuous data streams and bureaucratic records, these revelations would seem to be discovered accidentally through the players' cunning, not prearranged theatrics. And once uncovered, they would become part of the broadcasted narrative, impossible to erase.

Theron, leveraging his formidable combat instincts and surprising fluency with advanced systems, took on the most dangerous role: direct interference. Using covert access points secured during earlier challenges, he tapped into encrypted communications tied to the Obsidian Order. His goal wasn't just to listen; it was to manipulate the information.

He began injecting subtle disinformation into their channels, misdirecting their operatives and scrambling their coordination. It was a high-risk maneuver, skirting the edge of exposure, but Theron's precision and cold efficiency made him uniquely suited to the task. In the shadows of the game, he became a ghost in their systems, disrupting without leaving a trace.

Lyra, a surprising tactician of influence, focused her efforts on manipulating the narrative. She identified key figures within the Solar Concordance's media and diplomatic circles, individuals who could be swayed, even unknowingly, toward their cause. With surgical precision, she seeded compelling data leaks, half-truths, and well-timed revelations, subtly steering the perception of the Games.

Her brilliance wasn't shown in grand gestures but in suggestion, nudging public curiosity toward their carefully staged discoveries. Slowly, she turned the tide of opinion, painting the Obsidian Order as a growing shadow beneath the spotlight of the Games.

Kaelen, drawing on his diplomatic training, became the keystone of their resistance. He navigated the treacherous political landscape with calculated precision. Exposing the truth about the Order could destabilize fragile alliances and unravel years of tenuous peace. His task wasn't just to reveal the conspiracy, but to do so in a way that preserved order. He coordinated their efforts like a conductor, making sure each move unfolded in harmony, with impact and timing aligned.

In the quiet war room they had repurposed from an abandoned observation deck, Mira and Selene worked side by side, an unlikely pairing that operated with an eerie synchronicity. Mira, crouched near the central console, tapped through intercepted telemetry logs with the speed and precision of someone used to finding patterns where others saw noise. She didn't look up when she spoke.

"They've got fallback protocols. Shadow servers in the outer Jovian ring. If the Order suspects we're interfering, they'll torch everything and vanish behind a dozen false trails."

She slid a cracked datapad toward Kaelen. "We need to trigger the purge on our terms."

Selene, with her arms folded, watched the room with quiet scrutiny. Where Mira was sharp and kinetic, Selene exuded stillness. "Not yet," she said calmly. "We need the purge to expose them, not erase them."

Kaelen raised an eyebrow. "You have a plan?"

Selene gave the faintest of nods. "During the summit simulation, I'll propose an emergency vote, purely procedural of course. But hidden in the ballot will be seeded code. If the Order tries to hijack the vote, we'll be ready to trace the route back."

Her eyes met Kaelen's with cool confidence. "Diplomacy has always been a weapon. Most people just forget which way the blade points."

Mira chuckled dryly. "And here I thought I was the dangerous one."

Kaelen let the tension in his chest ease, just slightly. For all their differences, Selene's surgical elegance and Mira's chaotic insight, they were fighting for the same future. And in this war, he would need both fire and finesse.

The stakes could not have been higher. Failure didn't just mean losing the competition; it meant the collapse of civilization as they knew it. The pressure was crushing; an entire solar system poised on the edge of oblivion. Yet they stood united, no longer just competitors, but comrades bound by the gravity of a shared purpose.

They had crossed a threshold, stepping from the stage of spectacle into the theater of war. The Obsidian Order's shadow now loomed fully across the Games, but Kaelen and his allies were no longer playing to win. They were playing to survive, and to protect the fragile freedom of every world, not just their own.

The war room fell silent, its dim lights casting long shadows across determined faces. Beyond the glass, Helios gleamed like a distant sun, its arenas waiting to be transformed into battlegrounds of truth and justice.

Kaelen felt the soil pouch at his side, its familiar weight reminding him of the ground he was fighting for, the simple promise of home against the vastness of what they faced. He looked at his allies, fractured yet resolute, and understood that their unity had become more dangerous to the Order than any weapon.

When the summit doors opened, the stage would belong to them. Not as pawns in a game, but as architects of revelation. And once the truth surfaced, there would be no turning back.

# SHADOWS UNVEILED

They moved in silence now, between meetings, between simulations, between stolen moments in dark corridors. The burden of knowledge had transformed them, hardened their edges, and tethered them to one another with invisible threads of necessity. No longer just competitors, they had become insurgents in a theater designed for spectacle, conspiring beneath the gaze of billions.

Helios never stopped spinning, radiant and hollow, its brilliance masking the slow corrosion beneath.

The Games carried on, blind to the fire spreading beneath them. Challenges were still announced, scores still broadcast, the public still entranced by the illusions of fair play. But behind the curated drama, a different game had begun, one not measured in points or applause, but in secrets uncovered and time stolen from the jaws of a rising storm.

The trials ahead would not be won by strength or charm alone. Every step forward demanded precision, sacrifice, and, above all, restraint. One wrong move, one slip a bit too early, would alert the Order and invite annihilation.

The Diplomatic Negotiations challenge unfolded in a grand hall alive with shimmering holographic projections of the Solar System's many worlds. Terran forests interlaced with Neptunium oceans, Saturnian sky-cities cast long, shifting shadows across Martian deserts. The space pulsed with simulated life, an artificial but breathtaking tableau of unity and division. Every negotiation unfolded beneath a canopy of shifting constellations, their reflections dancing across polished marble like fragments of broken worlds.

Each competitor was assigned a planet to represent and tasked with navigating a complex web of simulated trade disputes, resource claims, and interplanetary power struggles. The illusion was elegant, but beneath it lay a test of political instinct, emotional control, and strategic finesse.

Jax, appointed as Saturn's delegate, was paired with Khel, the formidable Jovian miner whose gruff demeanor masked a mind as sharp as fractured glass. Their partnership, once grounded in mutual respect, frayed almost immediately. Khel's latent distrust of the Satori resurfaced early.

A distrust that was not brought on by accident.

Jax's manipulations were immediately effective. Carefully planted documents and subtly altered transmissions painted a picture both plausible and perilous. Trade agreements between Saturn and Neptune, seemingly benign, concealed hidden clauses granting Saturn outsized control over Neydrin resource routes. Encrypted messages between Satori dignitaries and Jovian councilors hinted at a secret initiative to control asteroid mining rights, at the expense of rival factions.

The language was bureaucratic, the implications buried, but to those with experience in politics, or suspicion in their hearts, it was like a match to dry tinder. The damage wouldn't be immediate, but it would spread. That was the point.

Khel, already predisposed to mistrust the Satori, quickly sensed a deeper pattern forming beneath the surface. His suspicion wasn't paranoia; it was experience. Years of navigating the labyrinthine politics of the Jovian moons had trained him to see not just what was presented, but what was hidden. And in Jax's planted agreements and suggestive data trails, Khel saw too many familiar red flags.

The veiled clauses. The strategic ambiguity. The subtle leverage disguised as cooperation.

These weren't coincidences; they were tactics.

Though his wariness remained, it gave way to something unexpected: respect. Jax wasn't merely playing the game; he was shaping it. And while Khel had little love for manipulation, he understood its necessity. Slowly, wariness shifted into a kind of alliance, one forged in mutual recognition of purpose rather than trust.

Together, they began reconstructing the puzzle piece by piece, unraveling layers of implication beneath the simulation's polished facade. With each discovery, the illusion of the challenge unraveled a little further, revealing not only the threads of Jax's strategy, but the shadow of the Obsidian Order behind it.

Days blurred together in a haze of strategy and scrutiny, each victory feeling less like triumph and more like defiance.

The Trial of Provision came next, framed as a logistical crisis: dwindling supplies across the outer colonies, shipments delayed, ration allocations contested. The competitors were tasked with balancing resources across simulated populations; each decision was tested against shifting variables of scarcity and unrest.

The exercise might have been abstract to some, but not to Lyra. She had seen famine firsthand on the Martian border colonies. The faces projected on the holo-screens of desperate families, angry workers, and soldiers guarding dwindling food stores were not simulations to her. They were memories.

Mira was the first to notice the discrepancies. Her hands danced across the console, tracing supply routes and shipment logs. "Look here," she said, voice sharp with certainty. "This freight schedule is impossible. They're shipping water to an outpost that doesn't exist."

Kaelen leaned over her shoulder, frowning as the data resolved. "Has to be a diversion."

Lyra's jaw tightened. "The Order."

The illusion cracked further as Lyra stepped into the fray, her voice rising over the chorus of simulated governors and councilors. She pointed to the falsified ledgers, hammering the delegates with precision: "You don't misplace ten thousand metric tons of water. You don't forget a colony's existence. This isn't incompetence; it's theft."

The room buzzed with uproar. Some competitors floundered; others scrambled to defend their assigned worlds, but the damage had been done. The planted anomalies stood exposed. Kaelen stepped in swiftly, tempering the chaos, weaving Mira's findings and Lyra's charges into a cohesive narrative that pointed toward systemic corruption.

For the first time, the crowd watching beyond Helios wasn't applauding a clever maneuver. They were witnessing the fragility of their own system, along with the shadow of those who had orchestrated it.

The Forge of Tomorrow challenge followed soon after, a test of ingenuity set in a sprawling laboratory simulation where each competitor was tasked with developing or reverse-engineering advanced systems. It was most definitely Jax's domain, but it wasn't clean.

His brilliance shone in the way he dismantled alien code, twisting it into elegant new patterns. Yet as he worked, Kaelen noticed the gleam in his eyes, not the fire of resistance, but fascination. For Jax, this wasn't just sabotage. It was art.

Across the chamber, the Venusian delegate unveiled a system too advanced, too polished to be theirs alone. Jax's eyes narrowed. "Sloppy," he muttered, fingers flying across his console. A cascade of data spilled across the holomap, revealing hidden subroutines laced with Order encryption.

"Caught you," Jax whispered to himself.

But where Kaelen might have tempered the revelation, Jax didn't. He projected the anomalies for all to see, his voice cold and sharp: "Venus just exposed themselves. Either they're getting help from the Order, or they've been bought outright."

The chamber erupted. The Venusian competitor sputtered denials, but the evidence was damning. Kaelen moved quickly, softening the blow, framing the discovery as a systemic problem rather than an individual betrayal. But the damage was done. The cracks widened.

When they finally got a break, they regrouped in their war room. Kaelen confronted Jax quietly. "You didn't give me any time to mediate."

Jax smirked, though the edge of unease lingered beneath it. "Mediation doesn't win wars."

Kaelen said nothing, but the thought lingered like a stone in his chest. Jax's brilliance was undeniable. So was his danger.

With each trial, the veil frayed further. Competitors whispered of corruption in the Concordance, of shadow games guiding outcomes, of truths long buried beneath spectacle.

By the time the final stages of the Ascendance approached, the Solar Concordance itself was stumbling. Scandal bled across networks. Factions armed themselves in the shadows. The Obsidian Order, though wounded and exposed, struck back with precise ferocity, its operatives sowing counter-narratives and subtle chaos wherever Kaelen's alliance pressed forward.

Their unity, once a fragile pact between rivals, had hardened into something unshakable. They had stopped playing for points.

The Games had become the crucible of survival. But beyond the arena walls, Helios burned brighter than ever, unaware that the Games it hosted were already ending.

The time for whispers had passed. What came next would not be decided by diplomacy, but by blood.

# BLOOD AND RESOLVE

The third trial shattered any illusion of diplomacy. Gone were the veiled political tests and psychological riddles. The ultimate challenge arrived without fanfare: a brutal public trial by combat. No more subtlety, only survival.

Even the air aboard Helios seemed to stop, like the machinery was holding its breath, as if aware that something irreversible was about to begin.

The competitors had known something was coming, but not what it would be. The silence before the announcement felt heavier than any simulation. Kaelen stood with his allies in the dim staging hall, the steel doors ahead of them trembling faintly with the force of what waited beyond.

The air smelled metallic, like ozone and machine oil. No one said a word. Lyra's hand flexed at her side as though itching for a blade. Jax muttered fragments of code under his breath like a prayer. Kehl rolled his shoulders once, the sound of cracking bone echoing in the chamber. Theron's stillness was absolute, a calm that seemed unnatural in its detachment.

Kaelen reached instinctively for the small soil pouch tied at his belt. The weight, a grounding reminder that beyond these walls there was still places worth fighting for.

When the transport dropped through the void, the viewports filled with a field of shattered light, fragments of broken satellites and dust orbiting a dying rock.

The docking locks groaned; the gates split down the middle, and the spectacle on the other side swallowed them whole.

The Obsidian Order had chosen a desolate asteroid on the edge of Satori-controlled space for the battleground. Its jagged arena, carved into the rock like a monument to cruelty, pulsed with engineered hostility. It was designed not to test strength, but to reward submission; to crush hope under the cover of spectacle.

But Kaelen and his allies refused to play the part.

Lyra stood poised, a blade waiting to be unsheathed. Jax's usual flair gave way to focused silence, hands calibrating his neural rig with obsessive care. Even Theron seemed stiller than usual, his stillness speaking volumes. This was no longer a trial. It was execution, with resistance as the only response.

The arena doors across from them shrieked open, and ten cybernetic killers advanced. Sculpted from flesh and machine, they moved with a predator's precision, their armor gleaming like bone beneath the searing lights. Their every motion declared a single truth: this was the Order's dominion.

Lyra struck first. She was a hurricane of motion and blade, weaving through chaos with ruthless discipline. Sparks trailed in her wake as cybernetic limbs severed from their hosts fell to the ground. Jax vanished from sight, cloak-field rippling as he slipped behind enemy lines. Systems faltered. Protocols scrambled. A killer turned on its own kind before collapsing in a tangle of sparks.

Kaelen fought differently. He wasn't built for combat, but necessity brought on by survival had reshaped him. He struck at joints, crushed conduits, ducked beneath strikes that would have shattered him to pieces. So long as he kept moving, he knew he could survive. Each blow he landed wasn't elegant, but it was decisive.

Theron was more surgical in his method. Cold efficiency marked his every step. He targeted commanders, severing coordination before opponents even knew they were compromised. And Kehl... Kehl was the wall. He planted himself at the center, absorbing punishment no one else could survive. His voice cut through with short, exact commands that kept the others alive.

Together, they became something the Order hadn't expected: a singular engine of resistance. Lyra's fury, Jax's disruption, Kaelen's grit, Theron's precision, Kehl's brute resilience, each part interlocked into a whole greater than itself.

The first wave fell. Blood and circuitry slicked the arena floor. The crowd roared, but no one among Kaelen's allies mistook this for victory. Their breaths came ragged, their bodies bruised, and before relief could take root, the ground trembled again.

The second wave had arrived; mechs, towering war machines plated in reactive armor, each a fortress of firepower and dark energy. Their cannons spat fire into the night. Their very footsteps shook the asteroid's crust.

Lyra scaled one like a ghost, planting explosives in the seams of its armor. Jax located a command uplink and corrupted it mid-battle, turning two techs against their own kind. Theron called out weak points with unerring calm, coordinating salvaged weapons' fire like a conductor orchestrating chaos. Kaelen darted in and out of the storm, planting charges with cold resolve, while Kehl wrenched reinforced limbs apart through sheer force.

Explosions ripped through the arena. Mechs toppled, thunder cracking across the stone. For a fleeting heartbeat, it looked like they had turned the tide.

But the effort had cost them. Kaelen saw it in Lyra's heaving chest, in Jax's trembling hands as his cloak-field flickered, in Kehl's blood soaking through broken armor. Their line was fraying. If another wave came, they would not hold.

Kaelen tasted iron and static in the air and felt that eerie stillness that only comes before a catastrophe.

And then the last gate opened.

The Obsidian Order's elite emerged. No machines this time. These were elite soldiers, sculpted through gene-forging and armed with cybernetics that pulsed like living weapons. They moved with an elegance that was terrifying, neither mechanical nor human, but something perfected for killing.

The air itself seemed to recoil. This was not about testing them. This was about erasing them.

The battle collapsed into chaos. The elites pressed in like a storm: blades clashing, plasma fire painting the cliffs red, the air filled with screams and the scent of charred metal. Lyra fought with elegant fury, every strike fueled by a lifetime of scars. Jax crippled enemy rigs mid-battle, his brilliance unraveling systems faster than they could adapt, though every surge of code pushed him closer to collapse. Theron cut through commanders, expression unflinching even as the ground ran slick with blood. Kehl was battered, bleeding, but immovable, dragging enemies into his own destruction when his strength faltered.

Kaelen fought without hesitation, instinct hardening into leadership. He pushed where the line broke, shouted where silence threatened to swallow them, dragged his allies back from the edge when failure seemed certain.

And then, finally... silence.

The last soldier fell. The final blow landed. The arena lay in ruin, littered with the wreckage of flesh, steel, and fire. Kaelen's chest heaved, lungs raw, every heartbeat a thunderclap in his ears. They were alive. Despite all the designs of the Order, they had survived.

But what remained was not triumph. It was clarity, sharp and cold.

This wasn't the end. The Order had thrown their best at them to crush them, and they had endured it. That boldness had exposed them. No longer pawns in a hidden game, Kaelen and his allies now stood in open defiance.

He felt the soil pouch once more, its quiet weight against his side, and knew what it meant: survival was no longer the measure of victory. The reckoning had begun. Beyond this asteroid, beyond the spectacle of the Games, a war older than the Ascendance itself was stirring, and this time, the Order would not be hidden by the night.

# PHANTOM SIGNAL

B efore the blood and fire of the Fourth Trial, before the arena became a crucible of survival, there had been a different war simmering beneath the surface, one of shadows, of whispers and doubt.

The blood on their armor hadn't dried before the doubt began to spread. In the quiet after combat, with the crowd's cheers fading into memory, silence became more dangerous than any enemy. Every breath sounded like a secret.

The phantom distress signal, almost forgotten in the chaos, had never been resolved. And now, in the stillness that followed the slaughter, its echo returned louder than ever.

The storm had passed, but it left behind more than scorched terrain. It had peeled back the last of their illusions. What remained was a wasteland of sharp, suffocating tension cloaked in suspicion.

Their truce, once forged through necessity, had dissolved into brittle silence. The phantom signal lingered like a ghost between them, a message sent from within, designed to tear them apart. No sender. No trace. Only the question: who among them had betrayed the others?

That question now filled every glance, every breath. Trust had become a casualty of war.

The room was half-lit; its walls still scorched from the last trial's feedback surge. Shadows clung to faces, deepening the distance between them even as they stood only steps apart.

Kaelen stood at the center of it all, no longer shielded by diplomacy or distraction. The mantle of leadership weighed heavier now, shaped not by tactics or charisma, but by the crushing burden of doubt. Before him stood the others: Lyra, pacing like a coiled weapon; Jax, uncharacteristically quiet, obsessively turning a scorched data chip between his fingers; and Theron, expressionless, unreadable, still.

The silence between them was louder than any accusation.

"It had to be one of us," Lyra said at last, her voice low and trembling with fury. "That signal wasn't random. Someone knew exactly how to place it, when to strike."

Her eyes drilled into Theron. Kaelen could feel the temperature shift, the tension ready to ignite.

Theron didn't respond. He didn't need to. His silence spoke volumes, and that absence of defense only deepened the unease.

"If we tear ourselves apart now," Kaelen said, his voice brittle, "we'll be doing the Order's work for them."

But the words rang hollow even to him.

Jax finally broke his silence. "She's right. There was a breach. Someone with intimate knowledge of our movements fed them information."

He held up the chip. "I pulled this from the comms relay during the storm. The encryption is sophisticated. It wasn't just hidden; it was buried behind a quantum masking protocol keyed to a planetary conjunction."

He looked up. "That's not a mistake. That's insider-level security."

Mira had been silent throughout the confrontation, standing just behind the others, her sharp blue eyes narrowing as the data chip's encryption unraveled. But now, she stepped forward, her voice low and deliberate.

"That masking protocol," she said, "isn't standard, even among high-level competitors. I've seen something like it before in Plutonian archival systems. It's surgical. Precise. Someone meant for this to be found... eventually."

She turned not to Theron, but to Kaelen. "You once told me patterns matter more than personalities. So, what if the real leak isn't Theron's detachment or Jax's paranoia... but someone clever enough to frame the frame?"

Kaelen blinked. "You think this was planted?"

Mira nodded. "Possibly by someone outside the team, but someone who knows how to exploit our divisions. Look at what this is doing to us. It's calculated. Controlled. And timed just after the Fourth Trial, when our defenses are lowest."

Then she glanced almost too casually toward the observation consoles. "There's a backdoor node near the eastern ridge. I noticed increased electromagnetic flux readings before the storm. It's low-band, has a Plutonian signature. If we check that cache, we might find the original signal's raw pathway."

She paused with a steady gaze. "But if I go alone, someone might erase it. I need one person to come with me. Someone none of us suspects."

Kaelen's throat tightened. "And if they don't want to go?"

Mira gave a ghost of a smile, cold and knowing. "Then maybe they're the reason the Order always seems one step ahead."

Time stretched as Jax worked, decrypting the chip while the others watched in taut silence. Theron remained apart, his detachment unnerving. He offered nothing, no explanation and no defense. And in the absence of clarity, the darkness between them only deepened.

"I've got it," Jax whispered.

"The trail doesn't name names, but it points to someone with access to Ascendance's command protocols. Sim access. Strategic alignment data. Proximity to the storm node before the signal went out."

His voice dropped. "It fits Theron's profile. Exactly."

Lyra moved instantly, her fury flaring to the surface. Kaelen stepped between them before she could act, his arm outstretched. "No," he snapped. "Not yet. This is damning, but it's not definitive."

"Kaelen," Jax said quietly, "the probability of coincidence is negligible."

Kaelen's eyes settled on Theron, searching for anything resembling guilt, denial, or even humanity. But the man was unreadable, a mask carved from stone. Kaelen's gut twisted.

Had he been manipulated this entire time? Or were they being played again? He muttered, more to himself than to the others, "What if this is the point? The Order doesn't just kill. It corrodes. It turns allies into suspects and suspicion into collapse."

Jax, digging deeper, found a secondary signal buried beneath the first, redirected traffic from a civilian comms node on Earth, filtered through bureaucratic back channels.

And then the final piece clicked.

A name flickered on the display; simple, ordinary, impossible... Silas.

Kaelen's breath caught. For a heartbeat, the room ceased to exist. The walls, the others, even the hum of machinery all dissolved into the weight of that single word.

Silas, the unobtrusive Earth administrator, the one Kaelen had known for years. Loyal. Efficient. Unremarkable. Not a mastermind. Not a monster. Just another cog in the system's machinery.

Except he wasn't.

Silas had used his anonymity as a shield. Hidden behind routine, he had threaded the needle between access and invisibility. He hadn't just leaked information; he had engineered a fracture, weaponized suspicion, and aimed it with surgical precision. The attack hadn't been on their bodies. It had been on their trust.

The realization cut deeper than any wound. Silas had been Kaelen's friend; a man he'd once shared quiet laughs in empty corridors with.

Someone whose advice had steadied him in early doubts. Someone he had never thought to question.

Lyra's rage faltered. Her eyes, sharp and merciless moments ago, shifted to Theron. And for the first time, she didn't see guilt, but restraint. His silence had not been cowardice. It had been about survival.

Jax sat back, pale and shaken, as if the weight of their misjudgment had stolen the air from his lungs.

Kaelen could not speak. There were no words for betrayal so close to the heart. The hollow ache felt worse than rage. It was like a brother's knife plunged deep, twisting between his ribs.

The revelation rewired everything. The enemy wasn't just outside. It had been among them, wearing a familiar face, standing in the blind spot of their vigilance. The damage was already done.

And in that devastation, something fractured, not just in the alliance, but in Kaelen himself.

The ideals he had clung to, trust, order, diplomacy, now felt like blades turned against him. The trials were no longer about victory. They were a crucible designed to strip certainty and leave only survival.

And even then, survival would not be enough.

As the sand settled over the Crucible's scorched plains, one truth remained: the Ascendance wasn't just a contest of endurance. It was the opening salvo in a war for the soul of the Solar System.

The Obsidian Order had only just begun. The shadows Silas had cast were only on the surface. Beneath them lay something far larger, waiting to be uncovered.

And in the hollow where trust once lived, resolve began to take its place; cold, unyielding, and ready for the darkness ahead.

In the hours that followed, no one spoke. The glow of shattered data cores cast shifting light across the room as Jax kept working, his fingers moving through the wreckage of code left in Silas's wake.

What he uncovered next would break more than trust; it would strip away the last illusion that any of them still understood the war they were fighting.

# SANCTUM OF SHADOWS

Silas's betrayal had been a blow, but what followed unraveled the last threads of illusion. As Jax peeled back the final layers of encrypted code, a deeper truth emerged—one far more devastating than a single traitor. The data didn't just implicate Silas; it exposed the skeletal framework of a vast, insidious machine. This wasn't the scheme of a rogue faction. It was a meticulously engineered network that had infiltrated nearly every power structure in the Solar System.

The war room was cloaked in shadow, its only light the pulse of code streaming across fractured consoles. Every face was lit by shifting green and amber hues, their silence broken only by the crackle of static and Jax's clipped breathing as his neural rig dug deeper. Each revelation fell like an anvil, with the weight pressing on them all.

Jax's voice was taut with disbelief as he read aloud the name embedded in the transmission headers: the Obsidian Order.

But the name alone didn't capture what they'd uncovered.

"So this isn't just whispers in the dark," Kaelen said, his voice low. "It's a directorate of officials, oligarchs and generals. Not bound by belief. Bound by leverage."

Beneath them, layers of sub-factions and regional directorates operated with chilling autonomy, each responsible for distinct sectors' economic destabilization, military infiltration and propaganda engineering.

The Obsidian Order was not a monolith. It was a hive of factions cloaked in unity, splintered and predatory beneath the surface. Power was fluid, earned through sabotage and survival. Silas had belonged to one such faction, a mid-tier bureau tasked with Earth's political manipulation and the orchestration of the Ascendance trials. His betrayal, far from an anomaly, was standard operating procedure in a system that rewarded disloyalty to everything but the cause.

To Kaelen, that truth cut deeper than Silas's lie; that trust itself had been weaponized.

Through Jax's decryption, the reach of the Order became grotesquely clear. Political bodies, media outlets, trade coalitions, and security forces had each been seeded with operatives who didn't just observe; they provoked. Financial crashes, trade embargoes, regional conflicts weren't systemic failures; they were deliberate acts of sabotage. The century of peace celebrated by the Solar Concordance had been a mirage, preserved not through diplomacy but through manipulation.

The Ascendance was never the point. It had been a crucible. More than that it had been an elaborate recruitment engine disguised as spectacle. The Order had watched, recorded, and selected. Those who could be converted were brought in. Those who posed a threat were eliminated under the guise of failure.

The phantom distress signal that had nearly destroyed their team? It was no random trap. Jax confirmed it had been deliberately fabricated using backdoor access only available to Order-aligned personnel. Silas had inserted false coordinates, timed them to intersect with a patrol zone, and created the perfect storm—a loyalty test wrapped in a death sentence.

But more chilling than the reach was the volatility within. The decrypted files revealed that the Order's internal structure was constantly shifting, a web of rival factions competing for dominance. Each cell operated independently while adhering to a single doctrine: engineered collapse. Power was not shared. It was seized.

And at the center of it all... Pluto.

The transmissions referred to it repeatedly as the Last Bastion. Not merely a stronghold, but a sanctuary. A world of eternal night, its surface frozen and hostile, its interior carved into a labyrinth of fortresses, research vaults, and buried archives. Kaelen pictured it as a wound at the edge of the system; black, festering, and waiting to spill into everything they had fought to preserve.

Some files hinted at Uthraxi ruins long buried beneath the crust; others at weapons sealed away since before the Concordance. Whatever the truth, Pluto was more than strategic. It was sacred. The planet was the nerve center of the Order's fractured hierarchy. It was the convergence point of everything built in the dark. Every betrayal, every transmission, every thread of manipulation traced back to it.

The implications were staggering. What they faced wasn't a conspiracy. It was a regime. A parallel power structure embedded within every institution of the Nine Worlds. Their enemy had wealth, soldiers, intelligence networks, and something far more terrifying: time. The Order had been preparing for generations.

Lyra's rage hardened into icy precision. Drawing on her Redborn training, she mapped the Order's internal architecture with ruthless intent, identifying weak points and potential turncoats. Her fury was no longer personal; it was strategic. She would dismantle them from within, piece by piece.

Jax worked without pause, buried in neural uplinks, decoding and categorizing terabytes of surveillance logs, asset rosters, covert operations. His mission was no longer survival; it was exposure. He would shine a light so bright the shadows could no longer hold.

Theron, his silence newly sharpened with purpose, focused on the fractures between the Order's factions. He traced chains of betrayal, exploitation, and internal sabotage, along with evidence of power plays that could be used against them.

"No empire divided this deeply can stand," he murmured. "We don't need to beat them all. Just push the right ones over the edge."

Kehl studied patterns of manipulation with cold fury. The Order's tactics mirrored the corruption he had battled within Jovian high society; dominance veiled as diplomacy. He began tracking behavioral shifts among the remaining competitors, quietly flagging those most likely compromised.

"We're still in their game," he said, "so we change the rules."

Kaelen bore the burden differently. While the others hunted threats and dissected networks, he moved among the remaining Ascendants. He didn't ask for trust; he offered clarity. Quiet conversations. Subtle alliances. He warned them without revealing the full scale.

"They're already losing," he said to one hesitant delegate. "The only way they win now is if we keep fighting each other."

Later, when the war room fell silent, and the consoles dimmed, Kaelen's hand brushed against the soil pouch at his side. Its weight was slight, but it grounded him. Faced with this sprawling nightmare, it reminded him of something simple: the earth he fought for, the promise of home against the cold machinery of collapse. The Order could plot for centuries, but he carried with him something older, something they could never counterfeit.

The solar system now teetered on a blade's edge. Their team was weary, fractured, and still trapped within the Games, but the illusion of sport was dead. They stood at the forefront of a silent war. The arena had become a battlefield. Every breath and every choice was part of a greater campaign, not for victory, but for the survival of the future itself.

They would drag the Obsidian Order into the light.

And when they did, Pluto would burn.

# RESISTANCE IGNITED

The weight of their discovery pressed down like Jupiter's crushing gravity. This wasn't just a mission to gather data; it was the opening move in a war against a hidden enemy so deeply embedded it had rewritten the very architecture of power.

The Obsidian Order didn't merely operate in the shadows; it engineered them, weaving false narratives, corrupting data streams, and manipulating financial and political institutions from the highest echelons of the Solar System.

Their first target lay beneath Ganymede's frozen crust: a fortified server farm buried within kilometers of ice and stone, its access tunnels choked with industrial scaffolding and abandoned mining rigs. Intelligence marked it as a central node in the Order's communications and financial web. Somewhere in those humming towers of data lay the threads connecting operatives to shell corporations that laundered assets across planetary systems.

Reaching it would demand precision, nerve, and total deniability. The installation was protected by adaptive defenses in the form of laser grids, automated drones, and biometric locks. The grounds were patrolled by Jovian security forces, many of whom were likely already compromised.

Lyra, leveraging her military instincts, devised the infiltration plan: synchronized diversions, a descent through Ganymede's labyrinthine industrial underlayers, adaptive cloaking systems to move unseen. Jax supplied the bypass tools and neural intrusion scripts, bristling with dangerous brilliance. Kaelen kept watch, the diplomatic instincts guiding their choices in silence. Every move Jax made with code carried contingencies no one else could see, and Kaelen couldn't shake the suspicion that brilliance and danger always walked hand in hand.

The descent into the tunnels was suffocating. Frost clung to the iron ribs of abandoned shafts. Their footsteps echoed against dripping ice. Above them, deep rumblings carried through the frozen rock as mining engines harvested other sectors, a mechanical heartbeat that masked their movements. They slipped like ghosts, cloaks shimmering against scattered light.

At one junction, Aris broke away without a word. Kaelen's eyes flicked to her, but he said nothing. She knew he noticed; he always did, but some tasks couldn't be debated.

The corridor she followed was narrow, carved from bedrock and lined with conduit pipes that hummed with current. The smell of ozone hung thick. She reached a surveillance nexus, a junction panel still hot with power. Her tools unfurled with practiced precision: disruptor, bypass spike, heat-dampener puck.

"This node links to six core observation hubs," she murmured into her private line. "Three of them tied to a Saturnian admin AI. Guess who's still watching."

Jax's voice crackled back. "You're sure it's not ghost data?"

"If it's a ghost, it's tracking us in real time. I'm not leaving it live."

"Keep it under ninety seconds. If you're not back by then, I'm yanking your signal."

"Then start counting."

As she injected the spike, movement shimmered across the polished conduit—a drone, gliding silently on magnetic tethers. Its sensors pulsed like glowing eyes. It pivoted toward her. Aris flattened against the wall, heartbeat hammering. The drone's beam swept across the corridor, lingered, then turned away and drifted down another shaft.

She exhaled in a shaky whisper. "Tell me you saw that."

"I did," Jax muttered. "You've got forty seconds."

Aris finished the injection, her hands trembling. The virus loaded with a flicker of cascading static across the panel. "This is what they used on us," she murmured. "False signals. Manufactured trust. The illusion of order." She tore the spike free, the system collapsing into white noise. "Let's see how the Order fights when no one's blind."

At the heart of the compound loomed the server farm: a cathedral of cold fire, its towers rising like glass spires, each humming with lethal knowledge. The air buzzed with static, light shimmering in fractured colors across reflective ice. Every step echoed as if trespassing in a sanctum.

Jax moved to the central console, neural rig lighting in pulses of green and red. His fingers twitched as though conducting an invisible orchestra. Firewalls fell in layers, holographic barriers collapsing into static snow. Kaelen and Lyra held the overwatch position, her weapons trained on every shifting shadow, her eyes on the catwalks above.

The trove they uncovered was staggering. Hidden in encrypted cores lay financial transfers disguised as mining subsidies, falsified diplomatic communications, and manipulated election records. Every stream of capital, every data relay, bled toward a single destination: Pluto. It wasn't just a stronghold. It was the staging ground of their empire, insulated beyond oversight.

Kaelen's pulse thundered as the files scrolled before him: trade accords sabotaged, security forces bought, assassinations disguised as corporate directives. The Solar Concordance hadn't been corrupted from the outside. It had been reshaped from the marrow out.

Jax's voice was hoarse as he finished the last of the extraction. "We have enough to expose the structure," he said, sweat running down his temple. "But not enough to bring it down. Not yet."

Selene's voice cut through the dim hum like a blade. She had entered quietly; her figure framed by the frozen light of the servers. "Then you don't bring it down. You make it collapse under its own weight."

Kaelen frowned. "You think persuasion will undo something this entrenched?"

"Not persuasion," Selene said evenly. "Exposure. You don't convince power to surrender. You make holding it more dangerous than releasing it."

Lyra's tone was ice. "And what makes you think the Council will even care? Half of them are compromised."

Selene met her gaze without flinching. "Then we exploit the half that isn't. Fear spreads faster than loyalty. Leak the right fragments, let them turn on each other. When trust collapses, the only currency left is transparency."

Kaelen studied her, seeing not just calculation but survival woven into her words. For the first time, he nodded without hesitation. "Then we expose not only the Order, but what silence has enabled."

Their retreat was no simple exit; it was a gauntlet. Sirens blared, corridors lit red, drones descended in swarms. Lyra moved like a weapon unleashed, charges planted to collapse pursuit routes. Kaelen narrowly disabled a turret before it whirred to life. Aris covered their flanks with precise bursts of fire, calm in chaos. Every second was purchased at the edge of collapse.

By the time they reached the docking bay, klaxons thundered overhead. Their cloaked ship roared into the frozen dark as security forces scrambled in its wake. The evidence was secure. The war had escalated.

Their next step would take them to Titan. Borin, a former Saturnian senator, had long suspected the Order's existence but lacked proof. Now, with it in hand, he represented their best hope for systemic inquiry.

Titan's skies were a storm of methane clouds; its cities suspended on seas of black hydrocarbons. In a chamber carved from glass and alloy, Borin received them. Lean and weathered, his voice carried the weight of years spent railing against shadows few acknowledged.

He scanned the data with trembling hands. His long suspicion hardened into rage.

"They've been bleeding us dry from the inside," he whispered. Then, louder: "But you've given us a blade."

Borin pledged to rally his allies. A formal inquiry would come. But Kaelen saw what Borin didn't say: the Order would not let it happen unopposed.

Retaliation came swiftly. Their ship was tagged in orbit, surveillance bots shadowing them across void lanes. Bounties spread through black-market channels. The chase began.

But they were no longer alone. Across the Nine Worlds, whispers stirred. Scientists. Defectors. Disillusioned politicians. Some had suspected. Others had waited for proof. Now they had it.

Resistance cells opened old safe houses. Data caches flickered to life. Clandestine transmissions carried a phrase like a prayer: We thought we were alone. We were wrong.

The journey through contested space became a symphony of survival. Ambushes by mercenaries. Dead drops in abandoned orbital stations. Voices on encrypted channels guiding them toward havens. Each ally was a flicker of light in the dark, tenuous but undeniable.

And through it all, one truth crystallized. The Obsidian Order was not omnipotent. It could have been fought. If it could be fought, it could be broken.

This wasn't about the Games anymore. This was resistance. And it had only just begun.

# RACE AGAINST TIME

The fate of the Solar System hung over them like a crushing weight, heavier than Jupiter's pull. Though they had uncovered only fragments of the Obsidian Order's grand design, it was clear the organization's reach was vast, its grip tightening with every hour.

Borin's support offered a tenuous foothold in the volatile landscape of interplanetary politics, but even his influence had limits. The Order behaved like a hydra: sever one head, and two more would rise. The countdown to catastrophe ticked louder with every breath.

Kaelen felt that weight in the soil pouch at his side. The simple gift from his mother grounded him, a reminder that this fight was more than tactics or survival. Every decision now was tethered to something greater: the chance to protect the ground itself, the fragile freedom of entire worlds.

Their next target was the Orders financial core: a vast network of shell corporations and hidden accounts stretched across planetary jurisdictions. Unraveling this labyrinth fell to Theron. His mastery of encrypted ledgers and economic architecture proved indispensable.

He traced illicit transactions and obscured holdings system by system, each thread exposing a deeper root of corruption. It was a race against time, demanding relentless focus, exacting precision, and iron will. The goal was clear: sever the Order's financial lifelines before its next move plunged the system into chaos.

Selene leaned over the tactical table as Theron's projections filled the room with cascading ledgers. "Money is their shadow army," she said, voice cold. "Take it away, and their soldiers starve." Her calm authority steadied them, the political mind reminding the fighters that data could cut as deep as any blade.

The investigation led to a remote asteroid mining facility orbiting Neptune, a covert hub for processing stolen resources and laundering illicit wealth. Infiltrating it bordered on madness. It was fortified, patrolled, and shielded by a defense grid no ordinary force could breach.

But Lyra, leveraging her battlefield experience, devised a plan: launch a coordinated assault of cloaked mining drones rigged with explosives while Jax infiltrated the facility's security network. Kaelen would lead the internal strike to reach the central vault and extract financial records linking the Order to its criminal empire. The risk was astronomical. Failure meant death.

When the attack began, it unfolded like a symphony of precision. The cloaked drones descended in silence, erupting in coordinated detonations that lit Neptune's blue-black sky with silent fire. Shockwaves rolled through the mining rigs, sending defenders scrambling for positions. Jax operated from a mobile command center, hands dancing over his console as he crashed surveillance nodes and unraveled digital barriers. Mira worked beside him, her smaller console glowing as she spliced overlapping channels.

"They're feeding commands through a Saturnian relay," she muttered, eyes narrowing.

"Same architecture they used on Ceres. This isn't just a vault; it's part of a spine."

Her words made Kaelen pause mid-step. If she was right, the Order's reach stretched deeper, more systemic, than even their darkest assumptions.

Inside, Kaelen moved through narrow corridors, bypassing laser grids and neutralizing guards with swift, practiced strikes. He hadn't trained for war, but necessity had sharpened his instincts into something lethal. The air reeked of scorched wiring and burnt oil, every breath thick with the metallic tang of fear.

Aris darted ahead of him, her compact disruptors flashing as she disabled drones before they could alert reinforcements. She slipped into a side corridor, her comm going silent, vanishing into shadow. Kaelen caught her glance back at him; defiance tempered by trust. She had her own mission here, and he would let her see it through.

The surveillance nexus thrummed with energy. Aris crouched beside the panel; tools unrolled like a ritual. A drone's shadow passed over her, its sensors sweeping dangerously close. She pressed herself into the darkness, heart pounding, as the machine hovered for an eternity. When it drifted away, she forced trembling hands back to work. Her injection spike slid into the circuit, rewriting the feed.

"This is what they used on us," she whispered to herself. "False signals. Manufactured truths. Not anymore."

Meanwhile, Theron fought his own battle in silence. His console lit with shifting numbers, spirals of red and green threads dancing across his neural display. Every successful trace revealed another account; another false ledger tucked behind layers of obfuscation. Sweat gathered at his temple as he spoke through gritted teeth:

"They're shuffling billions by the minute. Every delay costs us ten more trials. Hold the line, I need more time."

The vault revealed a trove of damning intelligence: financial trans-actions, fabricated audits, and communications exposing the Order's economic stranglehold on the Nine Worlds. The data was irrefutable, a digital dagger capable of collapsing their empire.

Their escape was a gauntlet of fire and steel. Automated turrets roared to life, and wave after wave of enforcers bore down on them.

Jax rerouted patrols and unlocked sealed exits seconds before capture, Mira doubling his work with precision reroutes that saved them from ambush. Laser fire stitched the air in lethal webs.

Kaelen pressed forward, blaster in hand, muscles screaming, each step carried by will alone. Lyra directed their advance with ruthless efficiency, turning every corridor into a gauntlet of survival. Selene's voice crackled once through comms. "Forward, not back. The world is watching now." It was more than enough to push them on.

They boarded their extraction vessel bloodied and breathless, but victorious. The vault's stolen truth now burned on their drives, heavy as destiny. Beyond the pitted windows of their ship, Neptune's cold storm swirled, lightning flashing deep within its endless clouds. To Kaelen, it looked like the Solar System itself, churning, vast, and ready to break.

# ASHES OF THE EMPIRE

Now armed with proof of the Order's financial conspiracy, the team turned toward their next objective: Mars. There, they sought General Rourke, a Redborn commander known for strategic brilliance and incorruptible principles. Convincing him would require more than passion, it would demand proof.

The briefing unfolded under the cold scrutiny of military discipline. They met in an austere bunker carved from Martian stone, its walls bare save for tactical maps and a Redborn banner scarred with burn marks from past campaigns. Dust clung to the air, illuminated in sharp beams of artificial light.

Kaelen set the drive down on the table. "This is everything we've pulled from the Order's vaults: financial trails, encrypted transmissions, chain-of-command structures. It's no rumor; it's fact."

Rourke's gravel voice rumbled like stone breaking. "I've heard facts before. Half of them collapse under pressure." He jabbed a finger at the display. "What makes this different? For all I know, you fabricated this yourself."

Kaelen didn't flinch. "If I had, General, you'd already be in chains. The Order doesn't waste time persuading its enemies, they crush them."

Lyra stepped in, voice hard but steady. "Look here." She tapped one of the maps. "Troop placements on Vesta. You trained me to recognize their formations, and these aren't Redborn maneuvers. That's the

165

Order directing your own forces against you."

Rourke's eyes narrowed. The room seemed to tighten around them. Finally, he turned toward Selene, who had watched the exchange in silence.

"And you? You've said nothing."

Selene's gaze flicked to the tactical board, then back to him. Her words were cool and surgical. "If you ignore this, history will remember you as the man who hesitated while the system burned."

A long silence stretched. Then, with a creak of armor plates, Rourke stood. "If the Obsidian Order has made war upon the Nine Worlds, then the Redborn will make war upon them."

With Rourke's support, the resistance flared into open rebellion. From Mercury's scorched surface to the frozen moons of the outer system, coordinated strikes crippled the Order's hidden infrastructure. Puppet regimes collapsed. Agents were unmasked. For the first time, the Order faltered. Its invisible grip weakened under the assault.

Mira found herself embedded in one such strike on Europa, crouched at a comms hub while Jovian rebels fired down the corridor. Sparks rained over her console as alarms blared.

"They've found us!" one rebel shouted.

Mira's hands flew across the keys. "Not if I shut them up first." With a keystroke, she severed the command chain. Enemy signals flatlined. She exhaled, whispering to herself: "Not this time. Not again."

On Saturn, Aris led a raid against a relay station. The detonation split the sky; the spire collapsed into molten debris. Captured miners cheered, voices raw with long-suppressed rage. A soot-streaked man grabbed her arm. "You're one of them, aren't you? From the Games?"

Aris smirked, tossing him a spare charge. "Not anymore."

And in the shadows of the Concordance Council, Selene orchestrated a leak. She leaned toward a nervous delegate, sliding a data-slate across the table.

"If this is true," he whispered, voice trembling, "the entire Concordance is compromised."

Selene's reply was calm, merciless. "Then it's time the Concordance stopped pretending not to see."

But victory had a cost. Each liberated facility revealed deeper atrocities: prisoners kept in stasis for decades, entire cultural histories rewritten, economies gutted and left in ruin. Kaelen was haunted by those they couldn't save. Even as planetary councils pledged allegiance to the resistance, he felt the weight of every loss pressing down on his chest. Dismantling the Order was only the beginning. Rebuilding a future from the wreckage would be harder still.

On Europa, Kaelen stood over rows of glass pods, pale faces suspended in time. His throat tightened. "Some of them... they've been here longer than we've been alive."

Mira's voice broke the silence. "And some will never wake. The neural decay is too advanced." Her hands trembled as she touched one pod, then pulled away. "How do you explain to a world that its family was stolen and left to rot like cargo?"

Lyra's reply was steel wrapped in sorrow. "You don't explain. You fight harder so it never happens again."

Later, in the ashes of a gutted mining colony, Aris crouched beside a wall of names carved by hand. Many were crossed out. She brushed away dust, her expression unreadable. "They tried to erase us, Kaelen. Erase everything." Her eyes met his, fierce and unyielding. "But we're still here."

Selene joined them, her voice low, edged with grief. "And the councils... they hesitate, even now. They pledge allegiance with one hand and clutch their old loyalties with the other." She exhaled sharply, shaking her head. "They will need more than proof. They'll need to believe in a future worth losing power for."

That night, in the dim glow of the Solaris's briefing chamber, the weight settled heavier. Silence stretched until Kaelen finally spoke. "Every world we liberate shows us another scar. We're cutting the Order down, but what's left behind may not be able to stand."

Theron rubbed his temples, exhaustion in his voice. "You can rebuild economies. You can draft laws. But how do you rebuild trust after this? After decades of lies?"

Mira whispered, almost to herself, "One truth at a time."

Kaelen looked around the table, taking in Lyra's quiet fury, Mira's fragile determination, Aris's simmering fire, Selene's cold precision, Theron's weary intellect, and Jax's restless hands. He could feel the weight of their expectations pressing against his chest. The war wasn't just about dismantling the Order anymore. It was about holding the Nine Worlds together when the fighting stopped.

When talk turned to Pluto, the air thickened. Kaelen stood at the head of the table, the soil pouch hidden in his hand, grounding him. "Pluto is the heart of it. If we tear it out, the Order won't recover. But we all know what that means... this will be their last stand, and they'll fight like it."

Lyra's jaw tightened. "Let them. I've seen what they leave behind: families erased, and children stolen. They'll find no mercy from me on Pluto."

Jax leaned back in his chair, forcing a grin that didn't touch his eyes. "I've broken their vaults, their chains, their signals. I can break this fortress too. Just... don't expect me to make it clean."

Mira's hands clenched on the edge of the console. "Clean doesn't matter. Truth matters. If I can get into their systems, I'll rip their lies out by the root."

Aris smirked faintly, checking the charge on her disruptors. "Then I'll make sure you live long enough to do it."

Selene's voice was cool, deliberate. "And I'll make sure the galaxy hears of it. Victory means nothing if no one knows what was destroyed

ASHES OF THE EMPIRE

in the dark."

Theron exhaled, weary but resolute. "We'll need more than firepower. Their factions are fractured, but desperation makes strange allies. If we don't use those cracks, they'll drown us in numbers."

Kaelen let his gaze linger on each of them. A collection of fighters, rebels and survivors bound by something stronger than duty.

"We end it on Pluto. For every world they have damaged. For every life they have stolen. Whatever it takes."

No one argued. The silence that followed was agreement enough.

Their last mission brought them to Pluto, the Order's last stronghold, buried beneath the planet's frozen crust. The fortress was a marvel of defensive engineering: stealth fields shimmered against the icy horizon, turret arrays bristled like teeth, and drones filled the sky in cold, mechanical swarms.

Lyra adjusted her rifle and addressed the strike team. "Thermal regulators go down first. No heat, no power grid. We keep them blind and cold."

Jax's voice crackled over comms from the operations vessel. "Copy that. Theron and I will cut the firewalls. Ten minutes and their network's ours."

Mira's tone was sharp, focused. "Watch for false recalls. They'll try to bait us into chasing ghosts."

Selene's voice was the calm counterpoint, feeding orders through allied cells across the system. "Your chaos here will ignite chaos everywhere. The Order won't know which fire to put out first."

Kaelen steadied his blaster, every nerve braced. "Then let's light the match."

The battle was cataclysmic. Rail-gun fire tore the sky. Plasma bolts shattered the dark. Shock troops surged through fortified corridors under Lyra's command, while Kehl and Jovian miners wielded modified demolition gear like weapons of revolution.

"Corridor B is open!" Jax shouted over comms. "Move, move now!"

Theron's voice strained. "Keep them pinned... just ten more seconds!"

Mira caught sight of Aris vaulting debris, planting charges with fearless speed. "Last signal's cut," Mira barked. "Kaelen, you're clear, go!"

The fortress groaned under sabotage and betrayal.

Kaelen pressed into the chaos, blaster hot in his grip. Explosions rattled the ice beneath him. Amid the cacophony, Lyra locked blades with an Order commander, her strikes fueled by fury. Kehl toppled a war mech with a jury-rigged explosive; the shockwave nearly knocked Kaelen from his feet.

The final push shattered the defenders. The Order's leaders fell, their command unraveling in blood and flame. The fortress collapsed into ice and ruin.

The battle on Pluto was won. The Order's network lay dismantled. But the scars were deep, etched in land and soul. Freedom had been earned, not granted; it was dragged from the shadows through grit and sacrifice.

As the smoke settled, Kaelen locked eyes with Lyra across the battlefield. Both understood the truth: the fight was not over.

The victory was decisive, but not complete. Whispers of a final contingency rippled through captured channels. All signs pointed to Helios, the final stage of the Ascendance, twisted now into the Order's last battleground.

What began in blood and deception would end in fire. And so, weary but unbroken, they set their course for Helios, ready to finish what was started in the dark.

# SHOWDOWN

The Helios Arena, once a gleaming monument to ambition, now loomed like a hollowed-out war god. Its spires shimmered under harsh artificial sunlight, casting fractured shadows across asteroid-carved corridors stripped of spectacle and cloaked in menace.

Once the stage for glory, it had become a crucible of survival. Emergency lights flickered along blackened walls, the air pulsing with residual energy, the ghost of battles past clinging to every steel surface.

Kaelen stood at the threshold with Jax, Theron, Kehl, and Lyra. Their breath misted in the cold air as the shimmer of advancing enemy forces grew on the horizon. The grandeur of the Games was gone. What remained was silence, dread, and the inevitability of the Order's final assault.

His fingers brushed the soil pouch at his belt, the rough fabric grounding him. A fragment of Earth, a reminder of where he came from, of what still lived beyond war. He let its weight settle in his palm before releasing it. He would need that strength now.

"There," Theron murmured, eyes narrowing as he tracked the horizon. "Not soldiers. Something else."

Kehl grunted, spitting onto the cold stone. "What the hell are those?"

Jax's neural rig flickered as he scanned the data streams. His voice was clipped, detached. "Bio-engineered titans. Executioners, not fighters. Designed to erase, not to win."

Kaelen's jaw tightened. "Then we hold the line. Here and now."

There were no theatrics. No protocols. What advanced toward them wasn't a squad but a force: towering titans of metal and flesh, each step exhaling death. They moved with eerie precision, not like soldiers but like inevitability. This wasn't a test. It was the endgame.

Lyra moved first. In her Redborn armor, she became momentum incarnate, pulse rifles snarling in lethal rhythm, every step a defiance of fate. She didn't fight like a soldier anymore; she fought like someone with no illusions about tomorrow. A strike ripped across her side, armor fracturing, but she pressed forward with brutal discipline, her rifle barking in controlled bursts.

"Lyra!" Kaelen shouted.

She didn't slow. "Stay back! Every kill I take is one less at your throat!"

Jax ghosted through the storm, Neydrin tech cloaking his movements, his neural interface alive with burning code. He infiltrated enemy systems mid-battle, scrambling comms, corrupting targeting protocols, sabotaging turrets. For a moment, his systems flickered, nearly overwhelmed by the Order's countermeasures, and Kaelen's stomach clenched.

"If I crash here, we're done," Jax hissed.

"Then don't crash," Kaelen answered coldly. "We hold because you break them."

The phantom recovered, weaving poisoned threads of corrupted code through the enemy. Their formations stuttered, movements faltered, cohesion frayed.

Kaelen pressed forward through the storm's eye. He didn't have Lyra's brute strength or Jax's digital precision, but he had resolve. Each step was survival; each strike a refusal to yield. Drawing on Theron's training, he calculated angles, environmental advantage and the art of necessity. He wasn't graceful. He was relentless.

"Left flank; watch their recalibration cycle!" Theron barked, voice cutting through the chaos. "Half-second delay on every second strike. Take it!"

Kaelen struck, blade angled to exploit the opening. Sparks and oil rained down.

Kehl was fury incarnate, every blow a Jovian hammer. His strikes cracked engineered steel where no one else could. A titan's strike slammed him into the floor, chest plate caving, blood spilling from his lips.

"Kehl, stay down!" Theron called.

Kehl rose with a guttural roar, staggering but unbroken. "Not... a chance!" He drove his blade through the machine's chest, wrenching it free as the titan collapsed.

Laser fire stitched the air. Explosions tore through steel and stone. Screams of dying machines mingled with human cries, a cacophony that made the very Arena tremble. The stench of ozone burned their lungs. Blood mingled with ash.

And yet, a rhythm formed. An unspoken choreography, born of fire and desperation. Jax's poisoned code bled through enemy systems.

"Turrets offline!" Jax shouted, voice fraying. "Comms are dead, you're clear!"

Lyra's voice was steel over comms. "Then push! Break them before they reset!"

The breach came in a surge. Jax exhaled and unleashed the virus fully. Enemy formations staggered. Orders clashed. Control chains collapsed.

"Now!" Kaelen bellowed.

Lyra surged. Kaelen followed. Theron and Kehl closed the gap, carving through stragglers. The fortress groaned under sabotage and betrayal.

At the Arena's core lay the command nexus, bathed in the crimson glow of failing data streams and hissing coolant. The stench of scorched circuitry hung heavy. At its center stood the Order's commander, encased in advanced armor, his face hidden behind a mask of glass and steel.

His voice boomed, mechanical and cold. "You are insects, gnawing at the edges of destiny. The order is eternal; chaos dies with you."

Lyra leveled her weapon, defiance blazing in the stillness of her gaze. "Then come and try."

He moved like a nightmare, engineered beyond human limits. His blows struck with terrifying speed and force, Lyra meeting him head-on. Sparks showered as her armor cracked, her grunts ragged but steady.

"Go!" she snarled between impacts. "Find his weakness!"

Kaelen circled, his eyes narrowed, watching. The commander's next blow hurled him back and made his armor scream under the sting of it. The sharp taste of blood filled his mouth as he tried to regain his footing. Every move was precise, calculated.

The commander was relentless, but calculations could be broken. Kaelen's arms trembled under a parried blow; his lungs burned from exhaustion, and his vision flared white from the impact. He felt the soil pouch at his belt. In its weight, he remembered: this fight wasn't for spectacle. It was for survival. For life.

"There!" Theron shouted. "Left joint, now!"

Through the blur in his vision, Kaelen swung hard, his blade slamming into the vulnerable seam. The commander staggered. The sparks cascading from his failing armor burned in the dark like fragments of a dying empire, brief and furious before the collapse.

Lyra roared, driving forward with a final, crushing strike. Steel screamed and split apart, shards of armor and blade scattering like sparks. The commander fell to one knee, a guttural sound tearing from his throat before he collapsed in a heap of broken metal and silence.

For a long moment, silence ruled over Helios Arena.

The battlefield had gone quiet, but silence did not bring peace. Smoke hung in the fractured air of the Helios Arena, curling through broken steel and shattered glass. The ground beneath them was scorched and cracked, a graveyard for machines and men alike.

Kaelen sat with his back against a half-collapsed wall, his blaster resting across his knees. His hands shook from exhaustion so deep it hollowed him out. The soil pouch at his belt felt heavier than ever, as though it had absorbed the weight of every life lost in the fight.

Lyra lowered herself beside him, her armor cracked and streaked with ash. For once, she didn't try to hide the tremor in her breath.

"You're bleeding," she muttered.

Kaelen touched the shallow cut across his temple and gave a tired half-smile. "So are you."

Their laughter was thin, but it was real.

Across the wreckage, Kehl sat with his helmet at his feet, blood smeared across his jaw. Mira crouched beside him, bandaging a gash on his arm with hands surprisingly steady despite the cuts streaking her own. Theron leaned nearby, arms folded, watching the smoldering ruins with unreadable eyes. He was already calculating what this victory meant, and what dangers would come next.

Jax slumped against a broken console, his neural rig flickering faintly, face pale. "Don't... say I never gave you anything," he rasped, forcing a grin that faded almost immediately.

Kaelen let out a slow breath and didn't argue. For the first time in a long while, he allowed himself to feel it all. The fragility of survival, the ache of victory, and the raw, impossible relief of still being alive.

They had won. But in the quiet between heartbeats, each of them understood the same truth: the war was far from over.

# REVELATION

The echoes of battle still clung to the air like a metallic ghost that refused to die. The silence that followed wasn't peaceful; it was only the pause before the next reckoning.

The aftermath of the Helios Arena was a ruin of scorched metal and shattered illusions. What had once gleamed with engineered perfection now lay broken, cratered by weapons fire and soaked in the stillness that followed slaughter.

The air was thick with the metallic tang of ozone and blood, as heavy as gravity, as still as death. Kaelen stood among the wreckage with his companions, battered but alive. Their victory was real, but hollow. The Obsidian Order's army had been defeated, but the shadow that guided it remained.

The looming threat coiled around Kaelen's chest like a vice. Survival wasn't enough now. They needed irrefutable proof, something to dismantle the Order's grip before it could regroup or erase its trail. The Interplanetary Council would not act on battlefield testimony alone. Its chambers were nests of political hedging and thinly veiled agendas. Only undeniable evidence could shake them into motion.

The search began in silence, broken only by the whisper of Jax's neural interface and the distant groan of the ruined structure trying to settle around them. His eyes were sunken with a haunted aura as he tunneled into corrupted databases, dragging encrypted fragments from the wreckage. Lyra, armor scorched and her side still bleeding beneath cracked plating, stalked the dead with blood-slick hands, yanking data chips from implants and examining insignias for pattern and code.

Theron worked with mechanical precision despite a deep gash along his arm, his stoicism masking pain. Kehl limped heavily, ribs straining under every breath, but his fists still clenched with purpose. Kaelen moved among them, his own lungs raw from smoke, every new discovery coiling a knot tighter in his gut. The air felt colder now, but it wasn't from the temperature as much as it was from the creeping dread of what they might find.

Jax's decryption peeled away the last veil. A sprawling communications network emerged, linking the Obsidian Order directly to high-ranking members of the Interplanetary Council. Hidden within those transmissions were coded authorizations, untraceable transfers, and deadly directives.

The truth hit like a punch to the gut. For a moment, no one could speak. Even the hum of the shattered systems seemed to falter, as if the station itself recoiled from the revelation.

Those sworn to uphold peace had been the architects of systemic chaos.

The Obsidian Order was not acting alone. It had been protected, nurtured, and unleashed by those in power. Kaelen's gaze lingered on Jax as the data scrolled on the screen, a fleeting thought gnawing at him... how much of what they saw was filtered or controlled by Jax's hand? The brilliance was undeniable, but trust was hard to muster.

Worse still, the Ascendance had been nothing more than a smokescreen. What was once believed to be a celebration of unity was now revealed as calculated misdirection. While the system cheered, the Order infiltrated. The Games had served as a forge, shaping killers, testing allegiances, and weeding out threats to the new order they meant to install.

Even Kehl, ever stoic, trembled with fury at the revelations. His fists clenched hard as he read the files, his eyes narrowing with a bitter rage. Kaelen felt it too, rage coupled with something deeper: betrayal wrapped in purpose. Every moment they'd spent risking their lives in the arena had been a performance, staged by monsters who had already decided the outcome.

Selene lingered by the edge of the holomap, her gaze not on the data, but on Theron. She waited until the others had moved away, their attention pulled toward the fragments of planetary intel now scrolling across the broken monitors. Her voice, when it came, was softly measured, like a scalpel.

"Some shadows, Theron," she said, "don't vanish when you step into the light. They just learn to follow you."

Theron didn't look at her. "Say what you mean."

"I mean the Ulen accords. The deal on Satori's outer rim. The informants who never made it to extraction," she said, letting the words settle.

"You operated in silence back then, too. The cost was always someone else's blood."

He finally turned, the lines on his face harder than armor. "That silence gave us leverage. And ensured our survival."

"At what price?" she asked, voice still quiet. "You made choices that buried the truth for the sake of control. I need to know you're not doing the same thing right now."

"I'm doing only what's necessary."

"No," she said, stepping closer, her presence a calm tide pressing against stone.

"We're not doing necessity anymore. We're doing truth. If you're still holding cards, if you're still maneuvering like we're pieces on your board, I will find out."

They stood for a moment, locked in silence. This wasn't open conflict;

this was diplomacy laced with threat... Selene's domain. It echoed her warning back on Ganymede, sharpened now into something more dangerous: she would no longer accept half-truths hidden beneath survival.

Theron gave a small nod, but his eyes held no apology. "Just don't forget who taught you how to play the game."

"And don't forget," Selene replied, "that I no longer play by your rules."

For the first time, Theron looked away. Selene didn't press the advantage this time; she didn't have to. The silence said enough.

The flickering holoscreen displayed a fractured map of the Solar System, each planet rendered as a pulsing orb, some burning bright with purpose, others dim with hesitation. Thin threads of light stretched between them, fragile strands of hope reflecting a growing collective will to rebuild. Kaelen's eyes lingered on the line connecting Earth and Mars, a delicate tether born from shared bloodshed. Lyra's words echoed in his mind: We fight together, Voss. Mars and Earth. Side by side.

As the data fed through decrypted channels and eyes turned toward war rooms and contingency protocols, the silence in the Helios command chamber stretched taut.

Delegates from the outer colonies, newly arrived in cautious orbit, began feeding signals of resistance. But the main council block had yet to respond. Too many still played politics. Too many still stalled.

Selene watched the momentum falter again.

She hesitated just once, the weight of consequence flickering across her face. Then resolve settled in like armor.

She moved to the center console and, without pomp, activated the wide-broadcast frequency reserved for council-wide emergency communication. It wasn't protocol. It was a precedent that was rarely used.

Her voice, quiet and composed, filled the chamber.

"We stand at the threshold of collapse. Not from invasion, but from indecision."

Heads turned. Even Kaelen paused mid-step.

Selene continued, her tone neither pleading nor forceful, but anchored in precision.

"After Helios, after the revelations, we now face a choice. Not between war and peace, but between paralysis and progress. The longer we deliberate, the more ground we cede to silence. And silence, as we've all learned, is where the Order thrives."

Her gaze swept across the room, settling on no one and everyone.

"There are voices already rising across the system. Scientists, diplomats, even defectors who've been waiting for the moment to act. What they don't need is another inquiry, another report, or a delay. What they need is proof that this chamber still governs with a purpose."

She stepped away from the console and looked toward Kaelen. Not for permission, but for amplification.

"I propose immediate assembly of a special oversight committee drawn from neutral planetary representatives. Mandated not to debate, but to implement. Evidence has already been secured. What remains is action."

There was no dramatic applause. No grandstanding. But the weight of her words lingered like pressure before a storm. One by one, murmurs shifted. Delegates leaned forward. Orders were given in hushed tones.

Kaelen exhaled. The tide had turned again.

As murmurs of support spread across the chamber in the wake of Selene's words, Kaelen felt a subtle shift. Not quite a victory but a loosening of the deadlock. The machinery of politics had moved. But it wasn't that moment that grounded him; it was the people beside him who had made it possible.

Once, Kaelen had seen Lyra only as a rival. She was formidable, unyielding, and a symbol of Mars' uncompromising will. But that rivalry had forged something far deeper: an unspoken bond tempered in the crucible of war. Together, they had survived horrors designed to shatter them, unearthed truths that unraveled the foundations of their world, and emerged not as adversaries, but as something closer than allies. Trust, once a battlefield between them, had become shared ground. In Lyra, Kaelen found not just strength, but clarity, a fierce sense of purpose that steadied him when everything else threatened to unravel.

And yet, their strength didn't stand alone.

In quiet moments, the aftershocks of Jax's work continued to ripple outward. The encrypted archives he had uncovered did more than expose the Obsidian Order; they revealed patterns. There were names, encrypted identities, shadowy contacts, and buried transmission routes that hinted at something larger: sympathetic voices scattered across the system. Scientists silenced for asking the wrong questions. Diplomats sidelined for pushing back against classified orders. Defectors who had seen too much and survived too long to be ignored.

Kaelen could almost see the faces in the flickering data, caught in half-lit transmissions: a scientist on Europa, gaunt and weary, sending scraps of forbidden research; a Jovian worker slipping coded warnings into smuggled comms; a Martian defector hunched over a broken transmitter, risking everything for one final burst of truth.

The data didn't just prove complicity; it illuminated a hidden resistance. People who had glimpsed the creeping shadow but lacked the means or the proof to stand against it. Thanks to Jax's findings, they now had both. Their message wasn't one of rage, but of resolve. They didn't need to lead; they needed someone to follow. Now, they had that too.

Kaelen felt the weight of that momentum beginning to shift. Their victory at Helios had drawn attention, but it was the undeniable evidence, the cracks in the illusion, that sparked real movement. They had not yet brought their case to the Interplanetary Council, but word was spreading. Quiet channels buzzed. Off-world envoys requested encrypted meetings. Unaligned factions began asking questions in public forums, breaking long-held silences.

It wasn't yet a revolution. But it was friction. And Kaelen knew that with friction one could start fires. Fires that could either guide the way forward or burn everything down.

Now, with evidence in hand and alliances beginning to stir, only one path remained: they had to take their findings to the Council itself. The seat of power. The system's last defense... or its final illusion.

As the chamber's lights dimmed and the echoes of Selene's broadcast lingered in the silence, Kaelen felt the weight of what was to come settle on his shoulders. Helios had been about survival. This would be a confrontation. Not against machines or soldiers, but against the most dangerous enemy of all, those who wore the mask of governance while feeding the shadows.

The war had shifted fronts. And the next battle wouldn't be fought in the shadows, but in the Council's heart, where light itself could be a weapon.

# NEW ALLIANCES

Their coalition was no longer just a handful of survivors clinging to purpose amid the ruins of Helios. It had become something larger, fragile and untested, but undeniably alive. Borin, a brilliant Satori strategist once skeptical of Earth's intentions, had been won over by the evidence. His decision to share classified schematics of the Order's weapons turned the tide of understanding, exposing critical vulnerabilities. Vahra, a hardened Jovian operative from the asteroid belt, brought grit and a steady stream of intelligence from the shadows. Her loyalty did not belong to any one planet, but to the people crushed beneath the heel of the Order's ambitions.

Together, these fresh voices shaped the outline of something greater than any one world. Kaelen knew how delicate it all remained. Centuries of mistrust didn't vanish overnight. Every handshake still carried the weight of old scars. Every agreement bore the sting of contingency. Progress came with caution, each step across a glass bridge echoing with the possibility of collapse. Yet it was progress, nonetheless. And progress, however fragile, meant change.

The days blurred into a grind of encrypted comms, secret meetings, and late-night strategy sessions aboard Solaris. Kaelen, Lyra, and Jax moved with practiced rhythm, each drawing from their strengths. The trove of uncovered information was staggering. They found sleeper agents embedded in planetary defense networks, compromised intelligence agencies, entire ministries unknowingly advancing the Order's agenda. What had begun as a single thread unraveled into a lattice of control that stretched across the entire system.

Every revelation hit harder than the last. The Obsidian Order hadn't just infiltrated power; it had shaped it, masked beneath layers of protocol and manufactured fear. This enemy could not be outgunned. It had to be unmasked. Truth, not force, would be their sharpest weapon. And to wield it, they would have to take their case to the one place where silence had done the most damage, the Interplanetary Council.

The Council chamber, once a bastion of ceremony and calculation, now crackled with unease. Delegates arrived draped in composure, but their eyes betrayed the truth: fear, curiosity, and dread all mixed in uncertain measure. The air felt heavy, thick with the scent of ionized circuits from the vast number of holoscreens preparing to ignite.

The chamber seemed to hold its breath, light glinting off the glass tiers like the surface of a calm sea before a storm.

Kaelen stood at the center, not with fire, but with clarity. His voice was measured, every word sharpened by purpose. He didn't just offer evidence; he delivered consequences.

He spoke of Helios. Of the smoke and silence that followed the collapse of a dream. He laid bare the Obsidian Order's plans, their infiltration, and the systemic betrayal that had turned governments into weapons.

"Silence is complicity," he told them. "And neutrality, faced with what we now know, is a choice. A choice with blood on its hands."

Jax stepped forward next, projecting decrypted transmissions that stretched from military offices to financial institutions and back to the Council itself. Lyra delivered cold, strategic analysis: the Order's supply lines, fallback positions, and command structures, all compromised.

Theron dismantled the financial web that had propped it up. Kehl said nothing. He simply stood there, scarred and silent, a monument to the cost that had already been paid.

Just as Jax projected another data stream and Lyra outlined the strategic threat, a soft chime echoed through the chamber. The central holotables flickered subtly, just enough to catch Kaelen's eye. From the corner, Mira emerged, fingers flying across a portable neural console strapped to her forearm.

"Apologies for the interruption," she said, her tone clipped but calm. "But we have a breach attempt in progress—it's traceable."

Kaelen's breath caught. "From where?"

Mira's eyes narrowed as cascading data pulsed across her display.

"Encrypted outbound packets sent from within the Council's own relay cluster. Someone is trying to siphon and scrub key evidence as we speak."

The chamber erupted in murmurs, voices rising and overlapping like a sudden storm. Mira didn't flinch. She routed the feed to the central projector. Instantly, lines of code and network pathways lit up the room. It was clear and could not be denied. A compromised Mercurian relay, piggybacking data through an anonymized link rooted in a Jovian commerce node.

"Whoever initiated it has high clearance," she said. "But they weren't as subtle as they thought. That signal is bouncing too fast... it's panicked."

Kaelen nodded. "Can you isolate it?"

"I can do better," she replied. With one last keystroke, Mira froze the stream and unmasked the originating encryption key.

The Council stared in stunned silence as the credentials flashed across the projection... an active Council member. The room erupted in gasps of outrage as security mobilized to secure the delegate.

The air crackled with disbelief; the sound of dozens of data-slates striking tabletops echoed like distant gunfire.

Kaelen felt something sharper than shock: pride.

Mira, who once hid behind systems and shadows, now stood unflinching before the most powerful assembly in the system. She had claimed her voice, and in doing so, cut deeper than any blade could have.

Mira exhaled slowly and stepped back. She met Kaelen's gaze with quiet intensity.

"I've seen the damage secrets can do," she said. "I'm done letting them fester."

The Council's initial reaction was venomous. Cries of forgery and manipulation echoed through the chamber. Accusations flew in every direction. Some subtle, others thunderous.

Kaelen stepped up to the podium but didn't end with fire. He offered a glimpse of something beyond retribution. He spoke of Mars and Earth fighting side by side, of Jovian miners shielding Satori engineers, of the possibility, fragile though it was, of unity forged not by treaty but by necessity.

"This isn't about territory," he said. "It's about survival and what we choose to become after we survive."

A few delegates demanded a recess. Others tried to discredit Kaelen outright, calling Earth's involvement opportunistic, its findings politically motivated.

But the evidence mounted. The transmissions couldn't be denied. The financial trails converged too cleanly. Faces blanched. Voices fell silent.

As the Council devolved into murmurs and frantic recalibrations, a tall, silver-robed Mercurian delegate pushed forward through the crowd. An aristocrat from the sunward elite, with his face burnished by photonic treatments, his voice was as smooth as glass.

"With all due respect," he began, eyeing Kaelen and Lyra, "our faction is prepared to support this alliance, conditionally. Mercury's interests, particularly in solar energy governance and orbital mining rights, must be protected in any future restructuring. We cannot rebuild civilization by tearing down the pillars that held it aloft."

Before Kaelen could respond diplomatically, Aris stepped forward from the wings of the chamber, her expression carved from salt and scorn.

"You mean the same pillars that funneled funds to front companies on Pluto?" she snapped. "Or the ones that watched Helios burn and said nothing?"

The Mercurian blinked, taken aback. "I... Miss Aris, I don't think you understand the intricacies..."

"Oh, I understand exactly what it means when elites show up after the fight is over, waving flags and invoices," she said. "If you're looking for a seat at the table, bring something more useful than conditions and platinum neckwear."

The chamber went silent. Not the silence of dismissal, but of impact. A ripple of unease rolled through the delegates. Some were appalled by her words, others quietly approving. A few suppressed smirks cracked around the margins, Lyra's included.

Kaelen gave Aris a subtle nod of thanks. She didn't speak often, but when she did, it left an imprint.

One delegate, eyes wide with horror, stood slowly and placed his Council insignia on the table before him. He said nothing. He didn't have to. The illusion had broken.

The ensuing vote was not unanimous, far from it, but it passed. A full-scale investigation into the Obsidian Order and the compromised institutions under its influence would proceed immediately. It was the first institutional blow against the Order, a fracture in a fortress that once seemed impenetrable.

For a heartbeat, the chamber stood suspended between triumph and terror, aware that the truth, once spoken, could never be contained again.

Names once revered were plastered across comm-feeds in bold red type, traitors exposed, reputations shattered, careers imploding in real time. Protests ignited across orbital capitals and city-stations. Some demanded justice. Others called for blood. The Interplanetary Council, once a pillar of order, now stood hollowed and cracked, its authority questioned on every world.

But the truth, Kaelen realized, did not bring peace. It revealed only the depth of the wound.

Old alliances fractured. Suspicion flared. Planets began hoarding resources. Local factions, once content to grumble on the fringes, surged forward to fill the power vacuum.

Even Earth, momentarily lauded for Kaelen's courage, found itself the target of whispered accusations. Embroiled by power grabs, manufactured evidence, and a push for dominance under the guise of heroism.

The council chambers transformed, seemingly overnight, from halls of diplomacy to arenas of political warfare. Every negotiation became a battlefield. Every agreement, a powder keg.

What had started as a mission to survive had become something far more dangerous: a crusade for justice in a system built on lies.

Kaelen and his companions adapted to the unfamiliar terrain. They were no longer warriors fighting for survival; they had become political insurgents navigating bureaucracy, deflecting sabotage, and building consensus in a system riddled with doubt. Their weapons were no longer blades or blasters, but truth, timing, and trust.

Lyra emerged as a steady counterweight to Kaelen's diplomacy, her sharp-edged presence cutting through posturing and delay. She confronted obstructionists with the same force she once reserved for battlefield adversaries. Where Kaelen persuaded, she pressured. Together, they made headway.

Jax remained behind the scenes, dismantling disinformation networks and disrupting the Order's communications lattice before it could be rebuilt. His data intercepts uncovered lingering agents and new plots seeded like landmines in the foundation of every major institution.

Kehl and Theron kept the coalition grounded, protectors as much as strategists. They coordinated security, vetted new allies, and ensured that trust wasn't blind. In every shadowed corridor and unsecured channel, they were the silent guardians, watching for cracks before they had the chance to spread.

The revolution had begun at Helios. But revolutions burn, and fire is indiscriminate.

Now came the harder task: rebuilding without replicating the tyranny they had just torn down.

Together, they stood on the edge of an uncertain future. Not champions of the old world, but guardians of what it might yet become.

In the slow churn of political recalibration, something unexpected began to take root. Delegates who had once dismissed one another as relics or threats now found themselves aligned by necessity. Tentative nods replaced icy stares. Private messaging gave way to open debate. The wounds of the system were still raw, but somewhere beneath the scars, a pulse of renewal beat.

Progress was fragile, but real.

Kaelen no longer measured success in victories, but in motion. He measured it in the gravel-edged voice of Vahra reporting another sleeper cell dismantled. In Borin's cool dispatches and decoded nodes of hidden logistics. In Lyra's tired but satisfied smirk after a council session that didn't end in shouting. In the silent vigilance of Theron and Kehl, steady even as the ground shifted beneath them.

The Solar System was wounded, not lost.

They had pulled it back from the edge, not as saviors or legends, but as survivors, people who had dared to stand together in the dark and strike a single match. Now, with that first flicker catching, they would guard it fiercely. Dawn was never inevitable, and shadows always waited for the flame to falter.

It had to be earned. And they would earn it together.

Yet as Kaelen looked out across the chamber, past the faces of allies and adversaries alike, he felt the tremor beneath the surface. The Order's roots had been cut but not torn free. Power was shifting, and the vacuum it left behind was already drawing out opportunists, zealots, and those who thrived in chaos.

The match had been struck. But in the shadows beyond the light, fire was spreading.

# FALLOUT

Across the solar system, the fall of the Obsidian Order's stronghold at Helios sent shock waves through governments, corporations, and common streets alike. The victory had not silenced the system; it had awakened it, leaving it raw and unrestrained.

Riots ignited in the Concordance capital as citizens demanded answers, toppling banners and storming council chambers. The arrests of implicated Council members should have been decisive. Instead, armored constables waded into the chaos, their boots echoing through marbled halls as power fractured.

Some officials surrendered quietly, their faces drawn with the grim acceptance of ruin. Others, deeply entrenched in their positions, resisted fiercely, clutching their authority with the desperation of drowning men. To Kaelen, watching it unfold, it felt less like reckoning and more like ruin playing out in real time.

General Petrov, the definition of a Redborn warrior, his medals dulled by age and smoke, rose from the chaos like a remnant of a bygone war. He orchestrated a covert resistance, rallying loyalist factions within both the Council and the military. To him, the scandal was a manufactured crisis, an elaborate ploy by unseen rivals to seize power. His voice carried weight in the barracks and the war rooms, and his actions plunged the already fragile balance into deeper turmoil.

Loyalist units seized comms relays and garrisons in the Redborn sectors, turning once-stable corridors of order into flashpoints. Skirmishes erupted across the Solar System as investigative teams clashed with Petrov's loyalists in shadow wars fought with equal parts propaganda and gunfire.

Earth, meanwhile, found itself dangerously exposed. Kaelen, despite his role in unveiling the plot, faced suspicion from factions that believed his family's diplomatic ties were a convenient cover for deeper complicity. Newsfeeds ran endless loops of his speeches beside images of detained councilors, planting seeds of doubt.

Pressure mounted on Earth's leaders to distance themselves from Kaelen, to sacrifice him politically hoping to calm down the unrest and salvaging their own standing. The conflicting demands of loyalty to family, to planet, and to the fragile truth he had risked everything to defend pulled Kaelen in opposing directions, threatening to tear him apart just when unity was most needed.

But the rot would not stay confined to marble halls.

The fallout bled far beyond the chambers of power. The public, stunned by the scope of the betrayal, turned their rage on the very institutions meant to preserve order. Riots broke out across the Nine Worlds, fueled by disillusionment and a hunger for justice. The illusion of unity and the carefully cultivated myth of a peaceful, cooperative Solar System lay in shattered ruins.

On Jupiter, miners demanded fair treatment and compensation long denied, their protests filling orbital docks with flames and chants.

On Neptune, tensions between the elite and the working class exploded into open revolt, violet skies lit with fires as domes once symbols of prosperity cracked under the weight of fury.

On Saturn, whispers of independence grew into roars as factions saw opportunity in chaos.

The system had not just cracked. It was unraveling.

The investigation spearheaded by the newly formed planetary task force began peeling back the layers. What started as an inquiry into the Obsidian Order metastasized into something far more insidious. Beneath it all was a web of secret societies, shadow corporations, and black-budget programs stretching back decades.

The deeper they dug, the more players emerged: silent power brokers, false allies, hidden architects whose manipulations had shaped interplanetary policy from the shadows. Each revelation stripped away another layer of illusion and left Kaelen's team grappling with a question more chilling than any before. Just how deep did the rot go?

The most dangerous of the discoveries came from the Helios archives: buried deep within encrypted data were weapon schematics and test logs. Proof of a technology capable of collapsing planetary shields, crippling defenses, even destabilizing planetary cores. This was no mere tool of war. It was an engineered apocalypse, meant to bend entire worlds into submission.

Kaelen felt the weight of it like a stone pressing into his lungs. All his years spent negotiating peace, preserving fragile balances, all seemed laughably naïve now.

For Lyra, the revelation sparked rage more than sorrow. Every soldier she'd lost now seemed a casualty in a war orchestrated from the shadows. And for Jax, the blueprints represented a personal violation. The weapon was a corruption of the very science he had once believed could unite the system.

Now, they stood not as champions of the Ascendance, but as the last line between survival and obliteration.

Kaelen bore it in silence, the weight of shattered ideals pressing down on him with every step. He was haunted not by what he'd lost, but by what he might still lose.

Lyra hardened her grief into purpose, channeling it into strategy and resistance, her focus razor-sharp and unyielding. She rallied soldiers and survivors alike, her reputation becoming a beacon for the disillusioned. She moved with purpose, a commander who led from the front. Her presence, a promise that they still had something worth fighting for. Yet behind closed doors, her knuckles bled from fists clenched in solitude; her pain kept buried so others could still believe in her strength.

Jax, fraying at the edges, turned inward, immersing himself in the pursuit of answers only code could offer. He fought from the shadows, his war waged across encrypted grids and dark-net archives. Every new breakthrough came with a cost: haunted eyes, shaking hands and sleepless nights. The scope of the Order's betrayal gnawed at him, but he didn't stop. He couldn't. Knowledge was his weapon, and he wielded it with ruthless precision, even as it hollowed him.

Kaelen battled on a different front. He walked the polished floors of fractured embassies, turning summits into tightrope walks. Each conversation was a duel of wits, each concession a compromise in pursuit of fragile peace. The old lessons his father had taught him, restraint, diplomacy, and patience, were now lifelines. But every word he spoke was shadowed by faces he couldn't save, and coalitions that frayed before they could be secured.

Kehl returned to Jupiter, to the mines that raised him. There, among dust and steel, he became something more than a symbol; he became a leader. He organized the workers, taught them how to demand more, how to see past the guilds and false hierarchies. But at night, in tunnels carved from pain, Kehl would sometimes pause, shoulders slumped against cold stone, remembering the cost of awakening such a people. And even then, he pressed on. Because to him, rebuilding wasn't a choice. It was survival.

Theron's path twisted beneath Neptune's illuminated domes. Once a pillar of controlled precision, even he bore cracks now. Alone in tall towers, his fingers drummed rhythms of unease as he sifted through the political fallout. He rooted out hidden loyalists, using strategy like a scalpel. But behind the calm, the betrayal burned. His pride had once insulated him from doubt. Now, doubt had become a blade sharpening his resolve.

Each of them carried the war differently. But all understood the stakes.

The Interplanetary Council collapsed in disgrace, replaced by a patchwork of provisional coalitions held together by caution and hope. Negotiations were agonizing. Old wounds reopened. Trust came slowly, if at all. And yet, against the odds, it came.

Amidst the grinding reconstruction, Kaelen and his allies found themselves, again and again, at the same table. Star charts spread out, strategies drawn in light and ink, the fatigue etched into their expressions like battle scars. In those moments, nothing needed to be said. The silence between them was full of understanding. Of grief. Of resilience.

They survived. And they would keep surviving. Not as icons, but as the scarred architects of a fragile, precious future.

For Kaelen, the burden had only just settled within him. Not in shouts or tears, but in silence, the quiet weight of a responsibility that would never leave him, even after the last weapon was dismantled and the last secret laid bare.

The war had changed its face, but not its stakes. Survival had given way to something heavier: the rebuilding of a system that had already tasted its own destruction and would never forget the flavor of it.

# THE HEAVIEST CROWN

The sterile white walls of the temporary medical facility pressed in on all sides. The sharp sting of antiseptics couldn't mask the deeper aroma of fear, a cloying undertone that clung to every survivor of Helios. Kaelen sat on the edge of the bed, the crisp sheets a stark contrast to the grime still embedded in his clothes, stubborn reminders of the chaos he had barely escaped.

His physical wounds would heal, but the scars they left behind cut deeper than any blade, silent reminders of what he had endured. The revelations, the betrayals, the near destruction of his home, they weighed on him like planetary gravity: crushing, constant, inescapable. For the first time, Kaelen feared he might not be able to carry it all.

His thoughts turned to his father, the man who had devoted his life to the fragile dream of interplanetary cooperation. That dream had cracked under the strain of the Obsidian Order's conspiracies, exposing truths Kaelen wasn't ready to face.

He once again saw the haunted look in the elder Voss's eyes: guilt, confusion, and a hint of something else... something closer to shame. Kaelen had long admired his father's ability to glide through political currents with grace, to defuse hostility with measured calm. Now he wondered, had his father truly been blind to the Order's reach, or had he chosen not to see, convincing himself that silence was a sacrifice for the greater good?

The question gnawed at him in the sterile hush, stripping away the layers of certainty he once thought immovable. Kaelen ran a hand through sweat-matted hair, the slight gesture betraying exhaustion deeper than fatigue. He was worn thin by the endless churn of deception and duty. He was no longer Kaelen Voss, idealistic son of a diplomat. He had become the reluctant symbol of Earth's resilience, the man who had dragged a system's secrets into the light and, in doing so, changed everything.

His fingers found the small soil pouch at his belt. He closed his hand around it, feeling the coarse fabric and the faint, crumbling weight inside. A gift from his mother, before the Games, before Helios. Her voice echoed faintly in memory: Never forget where you came from. Never forget what must grow again, even in darkness.

It steadied him in a way nothing else could. His father had given him diplomacy. His mother had given him roots. And in this war, he needed both.

Beside him, a datapad glowed softly. It held Jax's decrypted archive salvaged from Helios. Kaelen had combed through it repeatedly, as if repetition could bring comprehension. But the conspiracy was no coup; it was an infestation decades in the making, woven through government, corporate empires, and planetary defense grids.

One file stopped him cold: schematics for a weapon capable of destabilizing planetary cores and collapsing planetary shields. A chill spread through his chest. The scope of devastation was almost beyond imagination. A weapon not created just to destroy, but to terrify entire worlds into submission. The dream of unity, the carefully crafted illusion of peace, had been paper thin all along.

And somehow, through blood, grit, and sheer will, he and his allies had stopped it. Barely.

The weight of that realization hit him like a surge of gravity. He was no longer a participant in history's story; he had become its catalyst.

Thrown into the darkest corridors of power, forced to survive battles he hadn't chosen, he had endured when so many had not.

His mind turned first to Lyra. The unbreakable Redborn soldier who had become more than an ally. Once a rival, then an equal, now an anchor. In her, he saw strength not only on the battlefield but in the conviction that burned behind every command. They had weathered betrayal and loss together, forging a bond deeper than diplomacy could ever craft. It was trust, the rarest kind, earned not by words but by survival.

Jax followed: brilliant, mercurial Jax, the Satori technopath whose digital warfare had peeled back the Order's veil. Where Lyra shattered opposition, Jax sliced with precision. His intellect had saved them more times than Kaelen could count. Yet his greatest strength wasn't code; it was conviction, the quiet resolve to challenge systems built to crush dissent, even when it consumed him.

Kehl's face came next. The Jovian miner turned warrior, raw strength matched by a compassion he rarely voiced. On the battlefield, he had been their shield; in the aftermath, their conscience. His steady presence reminded them that even the forgotten corners of the system could produce giants of will and purpose.

Then Theron, the cold-eyed strategist of Neptune, whose precision often seemed inhuman, yet whose decisions had spared countless lives. Kaelen had once found his methods ruthless, but in time he saw them for what they were: necessary. Theron played the long game, and beneath his calculation burned a resolve to ensure the Order never resurfaced.

There were others too, without whom none of it would have been possible. Mira, relentless in her pursuit of truth, had faced horrors in the Order's archives and still chosen to fight with words and code when it would have been easier to look away. He remembered her whisper in the stasis chamber, trembling but unbroken: Not again.

Aris, scarred but relentless, whose fire refused to be extinguished by chains or shadows. She had become the living face of rebellion, proof that survival itself was defiance. He could still see her grin after Saturn's relay burned, soot-streaked and victorious.

And Selene, whose weapon had never been a rifle but words spoken with cold, precise, and devastating effect. She had turned whispers into confessions, secrets into indictments, until the powerful had no choice but to face the truth. The resistance had needed her subtlety as much as it had needed Kehl's strength or Lyra's fire.

Kaelen was grateful to them all. Their friendship had been forged in fire, hardened by sacrifice, strengthened by the kind of trust no war could counterfeit. He knew now that his own strength didn't lie in physical prowess or tactical brilliance, but in diplomacy, in weaving disparate elements into something tenuous but real. In navigating broken systems. In building fragile bridges between enemies.

But the scars left by the Order ran deep. The system's divisions had not been created; they had been exploited. Trust, the foundation of peace, was fractured across all Nine Worlds. Rebuilding it would take years, perhaps generations. And even then, some wounds would never close.

Still, Kaelen wasn't alone. Lyra and Jax remained steadfast, and new allies rallied behind their cause. The path ahead was dangerous, its outcome uncertain, but clarity had come at last. His reckoning was complete.

He would not let the solar system fall into chaos again. He would devote his life not to preserving the old order, but to building something better from its ashes. Not for Earth. Not for the Council. But for everyone still willing to believe that hope, once lit, could endure the dark.

He was no longer merely Earth's voice. He had become humanity's guardian among the stars.

But guardianship was not victory; it was a burden. And as Kaelen rose from the sterile bed, the datapad's glow still haunting the edges of his vision, his fingers closed once more on the soil pouch. The fabric was singed and rough to the touch; the soil faintly crumbling. Yet in its weight there was a promise: that even in the ashes, something could grow again.

The war for survival had ended.

The harder task—the war for rebuilding... was about to begin.

# RECONSTRUCTION

The aftermath of the Obsidian Order's near-successful coup left the Solar System marked but not broken.

Helios Arena, once a shining symbol of unity and competitive spirit, now lay in ruins, its twisted steel and scorched grounds a haunting monument to how fragile peace could be.

The arena's dynamic walls no longer conjured storms or jungles; they flickered weakly, struggling to hold form under patchwork repairs. Where holographic cheers had once echoed, there was only the low grind of welders and the murmur of engineers rebuilding one junction at a time.

Kaelen moved through the reconstruction zones like a thread woven into a fraying tapestry. Crews parted as he passed, some nodding with respect, others avoiding his gaze. He was no longer just the Terran envoy or a figurehead of diplomacy. He was the one who had stood at the fulcrum of collapse and kept the system from falling. That came with admiration, but also expectation and scrutiny.

The promise he had made in the sterile hush of the medical facility to build something better from the ashes pressed against him now with every step through these corridors of ruin.

He stood in what had become the Council's new center of operations, an improvised chamber deep within Helios's administrative ring, where marble and steel had given way to exposed cabling and emergency scaffolding. The room echoed with reconstruction, the very walls a metaphor for what they were trying to build: unfinished, unsteady, and desperately necessary.

Lyra leaned against the edge of the central holotable, arms crossed, expression hard as ever.

"We broke the illusion," she said. "That's the easy part."

Kaelen glanced toward her. "And now we try to build something real from the wreckage."

She gave a short, humorless snort. "Reckon it's harder to keep peace than to win a war."

They both knew she was right. Across the system, chaos simmered. Power vacuums cracked old alliances with minor uprisings on Ganymede, resource riots in the Saturnian Belt, and Neptune's fragile worker collectives threatening open revolt. Every planet had its own fracture lines, and their thin coalition was already stretched.

Kaelen had taken on the role of coordinator unofficially, as he was unelected, but trusted. He was the face that brokered the temporary peace and the voice moderating new accords. The Council had fractured and re-formed under emergency provisions, pulling in figures like Theron, Selene, and Nox to stabilize what remained. Each played their role with exacting precision, but the cost of cooperation became clearer with every passing day.

Trust, tried, and true, was still scarce.

"We need the communication grid fully online," Kaelen said, gesturing at the stuttering hologram hovering above them. "Direct planetary channels. Transparent updates. No more shadows."

"Transparency won't stop sabotage," Lyra replied, though she didn't argue further. Her presence at these meetings was proof of her reluctant belief in something better.

Down in Helios's maintenance levels, Jax had transformed a forgotten engineering bay into a neural-core relay node. Kaelen visited him in the evening, the two of them watching lines of raw data arc across floating displays.

"You're pushing the network into full sync with Saturn's quantum lines," Kaelen observed.

Jax nodded. "Integrating redundancies. Remote fail-safes on independent loops."

"And the Council doesn't know you've built back-door monitoring protocols, do they?"

Jax finally looked at him. "If we've learned anything, it's that peace is vulnerable and systems need watchers."

Kaelen met his gaze. "Just don't become what we fought."

Jax didn't reply. But he didn't deny the implication either.

Above ground, Vahra worked tirelessly on new extraction policies and environmental regulations. Her voice, once quiet in the early days, had become a thunderous force in post-crisis forums. Kaelen saw her clash with corporate delegates over Martian aquifer rights and Jovian helium quotas.

"You want stability?" She growled at the board of Terran executives. "Then stop stripping your neighbors bare and calling it trade."

Her bluntness earned enemies, but it also forged results. Under her direction, a new planetary audit commission was established, one with teeth and backed by interplanetary sanctions.

Meanwhile, Satori engineers released schematic after schematic: modular solar harvesters, collapsible bio-domes, vertical-farming pods adaptable to any gravity. What had once been secret guild tech was now shared with cautious hope, a gesture meant to rebuild trust through action.

Kaelen caught up with Borin during a systems inspection, the Saturnian technocrat pointing to a mesh of stabilization nodes.

"They'll isolate command-level overrides," he said, tone low and precise. "No more puppet protocols."

Kaelen studied the map. "I used to think trust came from open hands. Maybe it comes from locked doors."

Borin didn't disagree.

Then there was Aris. Mercurian by blood and now Kaelen's liaison to the fledgling security commission. She approached governance with the same economy she'd brought to the Games: direct, unsentimental, focused.

"We don't need symbolic gestures," she told Kaelen. "We need enforceable laws, streamlined jurisdiction, and above all, consequences."

"And if those laws fail?"

"Then we learn from them. But we don't wait for a perfect world before we start building one."

While the arena's reconstruction dominated headlines, the true test lay below the surface, literally. In the forgotten arteries of Helios, deep beneath the polished walkways and gleaming towers, danger lingered like a memory left to rot in the dark.

Aris walked the lowest levels alone.

No one had sent her. No official brief granted her access. But her instincts, honed under Mercury's unrelenting sun and sharpened in the crucible of the Games, told her something was wrong.

She'd flagged an irregularity in the maintenance logs, buried deep under system diagnostics and repurposed encryption. It was subtle. Too subtle. A fragment of code that mimicked redundancy, the kind designed to be missed.

She moved with purpose through corridors lined with exposed cabling and half-installed vent systems. Her light footsteps echoed, muffled by the hum of distant construction. Aris paused near a power junction panel. From a pouch at her hip, she withdrew a handheld analyzer... highly advanced tech, customized and silent.

The scan took seconds. The results confirmed her suspicions.

Behind the auxiliary coolant loop, buried in a maze of standard relays, was a filament-laced sabotage node. An elegant trap designed to detonate when the core systems hit full load.

It wouldn't destroy Helios, but it would spark enough panic to unravel weeks of diplomatic progress. Just a flicker of instability, a taste of old fear, enough to fracture what they were building.

She worked swiftly, her fingers as precise as a surgeon's. Within minutes, the trap was disarmed and dismantled, the components sealed in a containment pouch. No alerts triggered. No logs updated. Quiet prevention, performed by someone who knew the cost of silence.

Later, Kaelen found her on one of the upper walkways overlooking the cargo spires.

"You found something," he said.

She didn't look at him. "I found what someone hoped no one would."

He frowned. "You think it's the Order?"

"No," she said. "I think it's someone who believes like they did and learned not to leave fingerprints."

Kaelen studied her expression. She was focused, unreadable, cold in her clarity.

"We stopped the conspiracy, Aris."

"We stopped one branch," she corrected. "Beliefs don't die when you cut off the head. They go underground. They adapt."

He didn't argue. "Why not report it to the full council?"

She turned to face him. "Because this wasn't a debate. It was a warning."

And with that, she stepped away, silent, certain, necessary.

Those early weeks blurred into hard-won progress. Provisional council members met daily. Planetary charters were amended, ratified, sometimes thrown out and rewritten overnight. The new charter for the Ascendance, rewritten to foster interplanetary cooperation, became the symbolic keystone of the system's rebirth. No longer a blood sport or tool of manipulation, it would now host trials of unity: multidisciplinary challenges requiring teams from different worlds to win together or fail together.

The unveiling of the first joint team was clumsy and awkward. Comprising Mars, Earth, and Neptune, their strategies clashed, and their instincts collided. But Kaelen, watching from the edge of the chamber, felt something stir. Not perfection. Not even trust. But possibility.

That evening, he stood once more in the old Council chamber. The lights were low. The stars beyond Helios burned steady and cold.

He felt someone approach.

"You look like a man waiting for history to be kind," Selene said.

Kaelen turned. "I'm just hoping it doesn't forget how close we came to losing everything."

Selene studied him, then offered the faintest smile. "We didn't lose. And you're not alone."

He nodded... not out of confidence, but gratitude.

Behind them, Helios stirred with renewed life. Broadcasts resumed. Council delegates debated again. And slowly across the Solar System, something resembling cooperation began to take hold.

But even in that fragile bloom of progress, Kaelen knew peace was never permanent.

The first true test was already looming, and it would not come in a council chamber or a quiet negotiation. It would come in the arena itself, reborn as the system's crucible.

The same stage that had nearly torn them apart would now decide whether Reconstruction could hold, or whether the shadows waiting beneath its foundations would rise again.

# THE NEW CRUCIBLE

The newly reconstructed Helios Arena gleamed like a monument to hope, its curved spires catching the light of a distant sun. But even amid the brilliance, the shadow of the Obsidian Order lingered, haunting the system's collective memory. This was no longer about restoring a symbol. It was about redefining one and proving whether the fragile scaffolding of Reconstruction could bear the weight of reality.

From orbit, Helios looked whole again. Up close, it still carried its scars. Weld lines marred the once-perfect alloy. Scorch marks ghosted across the outer hull where the arena's defenses had failed. The light shimmered on new surfaces but couldn't quite hide the faint seams of ruin beneath. Every reflection was a reminder: beauty in Helios had always been rebuilt from destruction.

Inside the Interplanetary Council chambers, quiet deliberation soon ignited into fervent debate. For some, the Ascendance had lost its soul. For others, it had finally revealed its purpose.

Mars led with fire.

The Redborn delegation argued fiercely that the Games must endure untouched. To them, the arena wasn't just tradition; it was a crucible where sheer will was to be tested and leadership born under pressure. They cited precedent, statistics, even history itself, asserting that resilience was a lesson best taught through hardship.

Jupiter countered with pragmatism. Their diplomats proposed a reformed vision, one that measured more than physical prowess. They promoted strategy, diplomacy, and shared stewardship, pressing for a broader definition of strength.

Saturn presented blueprints instead of speeches. The Satori engineers envisioned simulations layered in complexity: multi-system crises, shifting alliances, ethical dilemmas. Competitors would be judged not on how many they could defeat, but on how many they could lead.

Neptune, as always, called for vigilance. Their delegates warned that reform without oversight was an invitation to corruption. Independent auditors, transparency protocols, and real-time evaluation metrics became their rallying cry.

And Earth... Earth walked the tightrope. Kaelen Voss, no longer a figurehead but the fragile spine of Reconstruction itself, called for gradual transformation. He proposed recalibrated metrics, transparent frameworks, and interplanetary review councils. His tone was measured, but resolute.

"The arena", he said, "should no longer crown victors. It should reveal those capable of uniting others."

For hours, voices clashed under the shimmering dome of the chamber. Every planet spoke not just for its people but for its pride. Arguments bled into philosophy, idealism into caution. The air buzzed with heat and static; the echoes of the old Games reawakened in rhetoric instead of blood.

When the final debate adjourned, Kaelen stepped onto a terrace overlooking the city's resplendent glow. Below him, Helios pulsed with fresh energy, construction drones swarming the horizon, light trails weaving through the dusk. But above, the stars remained indifferent.

Mira found him there.

"You're getting better at playing the idealist," she said, arms crossed.

Kaelen turned slightly. "We need something worth believing in."

She gave a low, tired laugh. "You say that like it's enough."

He studied her before speaking. "You don't think any of this will hold?"

She leaned on the railing, eyes distant. "It might. But not because it should, we're all just too exhausted to fight for something else."

Kaelen said nothing. The hum of distant engines filled the silence between them.

Mira's voice dropped. "Just don't mistake exhaustion for unity. The Order didn't rise out of nowhere. It rose because everyone was too comfortable believing things were working."

He met her gaze. "Then we change that."

"You're trying," she admitted. "But the cracks are still there. And the next fracture won't wait centuries."

She left him then, her footsteps fading into the hum of the city.

Kaelen watched her go, her warning lingering longer than the sound. Exhaustion, he realized, could look a lot like peace, until it broke.

Inside, the debates raged on. Proposals sharpened. Compromises hardened into policy. And slowly, a new vision took form.

The Ascendance would remain... but be remade.

There would be a new Council of Judges, with representatives from all nine worlds.

New trials, trials that tested diplomacy just as much as combat.

Simulations that demanded collaboration, ingenuity, and moral resolve.

Transparency woven into every layer. From scoring algorithms to public broadcasts, it wasn't just a competition anymore; it was a proving ground for Reconstruction itself.

Still, not everyone joined in the applause.

From the rear of the observatory, Aris watched with folded arms and narrowed eyes. She had refused her Council seat, refusing the comfort of legitimacy.

"I'm not here to be welcomed," she had once said. "I'm here to remind them of who they failed."

Now, as the chamber swelled with self-congratulation, she whispered to Kaelen beside her, "This system rebuilds walls faster than it learns why they collapsed."

"You think it's all a performance?" he asked quietly.

"No. I think it's survival instinct painted gold." Her tone wasn't angry, just precise.

"At least it's movement." Kaelen answered.

"Then keep it moving," she said, rising out of her seat. "Because the moment people feel safe, they stop questioning."

She stepped into the fractured sunlight filtering through Ganymede's stained-glass horizon. "Let them keep their seats. I'll hold the mirror. When they forget who they were, I'll remind them."

The reforms passed, and the Games were reborn. Not as a spectacle, but as a signal. A declaration that unity wasn't submission, but a shared struggle. That strength could be measured in restraint. That survival meant remembering, not erasing the fire that had almost consumed them all.

Applause rippled through the chamber, carried by the broadcast to every colony and capital. Across the Nine Worlds, crowds gathered before glowing screens, watching in wary silence instead of cheering. Even in triumph, uncertainty lingered, an echo that refused to fade.

Kaelen stood amid the noise in the chamber and felt the weight of what had been set in motion. The shadow of the Order remained, not gone entirely, only evolving. And this new crucible, meant to prove unity, would also become the perfect stage for doubt, sabotage, and betrayal to surface again.

The path forward would be narrow and uncertain. But it was theirs.

And in the quiet after the vote, Kaelen Voss understood what that truly meant.

The future was not a gift. It was a test. One he was finally ready to face.

# KAELENS LEGACY

The reformed Ascendance concluded without the thunder of combat. Instead, it left a quiet, lingering resonance that rippled across the Nine Worlds. Where once the arena's gleaming spires had stood as monuments to rivalry and spectacle, they now shimmered with a different weight. Testaments to unity born from survival, not from victory alone.

In the stillness that followed, Kaelen stood at the edge of the Council chamber's balcony, watching the final skimmers depart from the Helios Arena. What he felt wasn't triumph. It was endurance, tempered by exhaustion and underscored by something fragile and hard-earned: hope.

He found Lyra in a shadowed corridor overlooking the outer promenade. Her stance remained rigid, a soldier's posture etched into habit, but the slight drop of her shoulders betrayed something else, relief carefully disguised beneath discipline. For a moment, her eyes met his, and though no words passed between them, Kaelen saw it: the cost she carried and the choice she had made to bear it in silence, so others could lean on her strength.

Jax joined them moments later, his steps precise, his coat immaculate, the faint glow of his circuit tattoos pulsing beneath the fabric.

"We stabilized a fractured system," Jax said flatly, voice dry. "Exposed a centuries-old conspiracy. And didn't get atomized. I'd categorize that as a functional outcome."

Lyra arched a brow. "That's your version of a war story?"

"I optimize for low drama."

Kaelen smiled faintly, though the expression didn't quite reach his eyes. "We didn't just survive," he breathed. "We changed something."

Jax's expression remained impassive, but his reply carried more weight than usual. "Survival is just the first protocol. What matters is persistence. Let's see if this new 'unity' passes the stress test."

The banter was familiar, almost comforting. But behind it, Kaelen sensed what had truly shifted, Jax's sharpened protectiveness, Lyra's quiet pride, the unspoken current of trust that now anchored them. They had forged something no treaty could ever legislate: a bond built in fire and cooled in silence.

Later, Kaelen found Vahra supervising shipment routes to the outer colonies, her sharp gaze cataloging every movement like a commander still in the field.

"The reforms were only the first stones," she said, never looking up. "Now comes the harder part, convincing people to believe it's real. That this peace isn't just a pause between storms."

Kaelen nodded. "You believe it can last?"

"I believe it's worth trying."

Her voice carried a strength that hadn't always been there. It wasn't the armor of someone ready to fight. It was the foundation of someone ready to build.

Under the bio-luminescent domes of Helios, Kaelen later sat with Nox, the blue light painting their faces in spectral hues.

"We've glimpsed what's possible," Nox said, voice calm and deliberate. "Not through conquest. Through cooperation. And in that glimpse, I see a future where stability isn't enforced; it's chosen."

Kaelen met his gaze. "And if they forget?"

Nox's answer came almost as a whisper. "Then we remind them. Not with speeches. With systems. Structures that endure even when belief falters."

It wasn't passion that drove Nox; it was clarity. The kind born of silence and long observation.

The last voice Kaelen sought belonged to Aris. He found her waiting alone in the solar gardens near Mercury's memorial arch, surrounded by light refracting through crystal blossoms.

"We survived the trials," she said without preamble. "But we haven't yet survived ourselves."

He sat beside her. "You don't think the Games changed anything?"

"They changed us," she replied. "But the system? It adapts. The same hands that applauded the Obsidian Order now wear reform like a cloak. It's not justice; it's camouflage."

Kaelen didn't argue. He simply let the silence stretch, understanding that Aris wasn't there to condemn hope, but to guard it.

"I'm not here to be part of the Council," she continued. "I'm here to watch. To remember. To make sure none of you forget what darkness looked like before the lights came back on."

In her gaze, Kaelen saw something fierce and irreplaceable. Not distrust. Not bitterness. But vigilance. The kind the new system would need to stay honest.

Elsewhere, Kehl had returned to Jupiter's mining domes, standing not just as a fighter but as a leader among his people. His reports were full of hard work and harder truths. Organizing workers, demanding their fair treatment, and teaching them to see their worth.

Theron, meanwhile, had positioned himself within Neptune's new oversight corps, his strategic precision turned toward rooting out hidden loyalists before they could fracture what had barely been repaired. Neither sought the spotlight, but their shadows stretched long across the fragile peace.

Over the following months, the bond between the former competitors solidified into something deeper: an unspoken alliance. They met regularly to coordinate policy, but most of all to keep each other grounded.

Stories were shared, and warnings exchanged. Progress celebrated in minor victories: a water-sharing treaty on Europa, a new trade corridor through the Belt, a medical exchange co-funded by rival worlds.

Together, they guided the fragile solar peace like navigators watching the stars. Steering by light, not by force.

The re-imagined Ascendance became not just a crucible for emerging leaders, but a symbol of what could be achieved when unity was forged in hardship and tempered by trust. Each new cycle brought competitors not to win, but to collaborate, to learn, to carry forward the ideals Kaelen and his allies had fought to defend.

On a quiet evening, Kaelen stood beneath the stars, far from the cameras and council halls. The silver horizon of Ganymede stretched wide before him, unscarred and vast. In his palm, the small soil pouch his mother had once given him felt warm against the chill air. He held it lightly, not as a relic, but as a reminder that resilience begins in the smallest of things.

He breathed in the stillness. The war was over. The Order was defeated. But the actual work... this work... was only beginning.

He thought of the bonds now anchoring the Nine Worlds. Of the fire-forged friendships that refused to die: Lyra's resolve, Jax's quiet brilliance, Vahra's strength, Nox's logic, Aris's vigilance, Kehl and Theron's steady guardianship.

This, he realized, was the true legacy. Not power. Not reputation. But connection. A web strong enough to hold even when the system shook.

And as the stars blinked above him, Kaelen understood this to be true: so long as those bonds endured, the future wasn't just possible; it was inevitable. It was his legacy, carried forward in the hands of many, a burden shared, and a light guarded together.

# A NEW ERA

The echoes of triumph had faded, replaced by the slow, methodical rhythm of rebuilding. In the halls of the Interplanetary Council, what once pulsed with rivalry now thrummed with deliberation, compromise, and the grinding machinery of governance. The unity forged in crisis had become something more fragile, an experiment in cooperation that demanded constant tending.

Kaelen Voss moved through it all like a man carrying a torch through a storm, aware of how quickly the flame could sputter out.

He no longer fought for survival. He fought for permanence.

The first step had been to hope, as trust could easily be fractured, tentative and elusive. The Order had not merely corrupted systems; it had infected perception itself. Every gesture of collaboration now had to swim against decades of suspicion. Still, Kaelen pressed forward, spearheading a communications initiative that linked the Nine Worlds through immersive, real-time dialogue. Holographic relays stitched the void with light, binding planetary parliaments in shared transparency.

Most nights, Kaelen lingered after the chambers emptied, watching those connections flicker between worlds. Sometimes he caught a spark of hope in an unexpected handshake. Other times there was only silence. And he wondered, would it hold?

Selene found him during one such night, her footsteps soft against the polished stone.

"You're building something remarkable," she said. "But it's balanced on a pinhead."

He didn't turn. "You think it will fall."

"I think memory is longer than policy," she replied. "Unity asks us to forget the lines we once defended. And most people aren't ready to forget."

He turned toward her, his brow tight. "So, we walk on eggshells forever?"

"No," she said, stepping beside him. "You walk like a diplomat and think like a strategist. Let the other worlds feel their own strength in this new order, even if you're the one holding the frame together."

Her gaze drifted to the emblems above the council seats. "Let them win. Quietly. Proudly. That's how you keep this alive."

Her words settled like dust in the quiet—not a threat, but truth. Then she turned and left him alone with the hum of distant engines.

Lyra's vision was simpler, and perhaps stronger as well. She forged ahead with the creation of a joint interplanetary defense force, her Redborn discipline turning shared struggle into the language of trust. Kaelen watched soldiers from rival planets train together under her command, shoulder to shoulder, not in battle but in purpose. In every synchronized maneuver, he saw hope take physical form.

Theron, the tactician that he was, moved through treaty rooms like a conductor, shaping accords that balanced not power but equity, negotiating mining rights, trade corridors, and environmental reparations. His calm precision reminded Kaelen that peace wasn't an ideal. It was a structure that could be drafted, ratified, and defended.

Vahra grounded it all. Her work ensured that prosperity would not become exploitation. She fought for sustainable mining, renewable energy, and the restoration of damaged ecosystems. One evening, as they stood together in a Helios shipping bay watching cargo modules drift like silver embers, she spoke without looking at him.

"You ever wonder if we've just painted over the cracks?"

Kaelen glanced at her. "You think it's not enough?"

She shrugged. "We passed laws and built systems. But I still hear them whisper, the ones who admired the Order. They're not gone, just quieter."

He met her eyes. "You think they'll rise again?"

"Eventually," she said. "Ideology doesn't die. It just sleeps."

She paused, her tone softening. "Just promise me we won't be too proud to see it when it wakes."

Jax remained their ghost in the machine. Kaelen often found him deep in the neural networks, decrypting anomalies, tracing the data undercurrents others ignored. Once, Kaelen joined him at a viewport overlooking the Helios perimeter.

"You're still expecting sabotage?" Kaelen asked.

Jax gave a tired smile. "I expect entropy. Everything breaks eventually. Our job is to hold it together longer than they expect."

Kaelen clasped his shoulder. "Then don't stop watching."

Even Borin, quiet and meticulous Borin, had become a bulwark. His overhaul of Saturn's infrastructure hardened the system against future manipulation.

"The Order used our blindness against us," he told Kaelen. "Now we watch everything. And we remember."

The Ascendance grew too. No longer a contest of dominance, it became a crucible of collaboration. Multi-planetary teams faced diplomatic simulations, crisis-response trials, and feats of shared innovation. Cultural festivals bloomed alongside them, full of Jovian sky dances, Martian storytelling, and Saturnian light-sculpture exhibitions. The Games had become a more of a rehearsal for the future, not a test of supremacy.

Still, old wounds lingered. Economic tensions flared. Prejudices resurfaced. But this time, they had tools in the form of mediation councils, cultural exchanges, and fair trade charters. And, more importantly, they had each other.

Kaelen often walked the corridors of Helios late at night, music and laughter echoing from open doors. One evening, he paused on the observation deck. Diplomatic shuttles and freighters crossed the void below, each light a fragile thread in the tapestry of peace.

On the far edge of a sensor grid, he noticed a flicker. Static, the technicians told him. A ghost glitch more than likely.

But something in his chest tightened at the sight of it. The Order's shadow had not vanished. It had only been absorbed in vigilance.

He exhaled, steadying himself, trying to banish the whisper that the veritable storms had yet to come. When he opened his eyes again, the stars stared back, cold, patient, and indifferent.

Still, he stayed.

Still, he watched.

The future wasn't guaranteed. But it was real.

And it was theirs to shape.

Kaelen remained on the deck long after the Council chambers dimmed to silence. Below, Helios shimmered with the flicker of new life. Trade ships threading cautious routes, beacons pulsing across the void, and the voices of Nine Worlds stitched together through fragile channels. It looked like peace. It even felt like it, if only for a heartbeat.

Yet beyond the lights, the stars burned cold and far away, their silence heavier than applause. Kaelen rested his hand against the viewport, feeling the tremor of engines, the hum of rebuilt systems. They had survived the Order and rewritten the Games. They had proven that unity was possible. But deep in his chest, he knew the truth no decree could erase... survival was not permanence.

Peace had been bought but not secured.

And somewhere in that vast dark void, something was still watching.

Kaelen exhaled, letting the release of his breath center him. The future was not a prize to be claimed; it was a burden to be carried. Whatever storms came next, whatever shadows rose from the void, they would be met as Helios had been saved... together.

For now, the Nine Worlds could breathe. For now, hope endured.

But Kaelen Voss knew one immutable truth: history never sleeps for long.

# About the Author

Rocky has always been fascinated by the stars. From growing up in a military family, to his own career in the United States Air Force that carried him across every hemisphere of the Earth, he has lived a life of exploration. That same spirit led him to imagine: what if every world in our solar system was alive with people, rife with power, and conflict? The answer became Shadow of Helios, his debut novel and the first in a planned four-book series. Inspired by the epic scope of Dune and The Expanse and the raw intensity of Red Rising and The Hunger Games, he writes stories of survival, betrayal, and fragile unity. When not building worlds on the page, he can be found hiking trails, discovering new places, and, like Kaelen Voss, carrying his curiosity into uncharted territory.

**You can connect with me on:**

[f] https://www.facebook.com/profile.php?id=61582690104994